NEVER SAY QUIT

NEVER SAY QUIT

●●●

Bill Wallace

Holiday House/New York

Copyright © 1993 by Bill Wallace
Printed in the United States of America
All rights reserved
First Edition

Library of Congress Cataloging-in-Publication Data
Wallace, Bill, 1947–
Never say quit / Bill Wallace.
p.   cm.
Summary: Angry when they are excluded from the soccer team, sixth
grader Justine and the rest of the school misfits form their own team and
begin training with a coach who drinks heavily but gives them a
special gift.
ISBN 0-8234-1013-7
[1. Soccer—Fiction.   2. Alcoholism—Fiction.]   I. Title.
PZ7.W15473Ne   1993   92-54420   CIP   AC
[Fic]—dc20

To Nikki and the Chickasha Youth Soccer Association's under-nineteen girls teams of 1990, 1991, and 1992,

and

to Justin and the Chickasha Youth Soccer Association's under-sixteen boys teams of 1989 and 1990, and the under-nineteen boys teams of 1991 and 1992.

NEVER SAY QUIT

CHAPTER 1

We were the leftovers. The scrubs. There were seven of us—four boys and three girls. The seven who nobody wanted.

That was fine with me!

So what if I wasn't very good? So what if the ball didn't always roll where I kicked it? So what if I tripped over my own big feet or forgot and used my hands sometimes? I didn't care!

Only, I really did.

It was chilly in the library meeting room where the two soccer coaches were picking the team. I cupped my hands under my bare elbows. They were cold as ice.

"It's not fair."

Billy Queen walked over and ruffled my hair.

"Sorry, hon," he said with a smile. The thin mustache on his upper lip and his scrawny eyebrows gave him a sneaky look. "If we had another coach and a few more players . . . well . . . you understand, don't you?"

I ducked my head away from his hand and brushed his touch from my long hair.

"Sure!"

He smiled again, and that sneaky mustache curled higher.

"It's not that you aren't sweet kids. It's not that at all. It's just . . . well, we only have one coach and one assistant coach. We can only have eighteen kids on the roster and . . . well . . ."

Randy Black looked down at his hands and started counting his fingers.

"It's because I can't buy shin guards or stuff," Kathy Fields said.

"I'm too little." My brother Nick stepped up next to me.

"It's because I'm black," Jerry Tate pouted.

"I'm clumsy." Brandon Foreman towered above Nick as he moved beside us.

Paula Liven tried to help out Coach Queen.

"Now, children," she soothed, "we'd love to have you on the team . . ." Paula Liven had the sweetest voice. The way she fluttered her long, fake eye-

lashes and wiggled around made me want to barf.
". . . it's just that we don't have room."

The folding chair Randy Black was sitting on
squeaked when he leaned to the side. Whatever he
was trying to count on his fingers wasn't working, so
he traced the numbers in the plush pile carpet.

"It's not fair," I mumbled again.

"Now, Justine." Paula Liven smiled. "You're such
a sweet, pretty girl. It's not becoming of you to . . ."

Her voice was like a drippy-sweet pop that somebody had forgotten to put the carbonated water in—
all syrupy and gooey, but with no fizz or life to it.

"It's just that we aren't any good," Nick grumped.
His bottom lip drooped low. "If we were like the
other kids, they'd let us play."

"Oh, no, dear." Paula's voice was still dripping.
"Your soccer skills have come along fine, you've
improved, just like the other kids. It's just that . . .
well . . ."

Paula Liven was as good a liar as Billy Queen.
Probably better. Now, even she was having trouble
getting out of this one.

"Your skills have improved a great deal. You simply don't have the experience that some of the other
kids do. I mean, some of these boys and girls have
played together since kindergarten. They've played
indoor soccer during the off-season and they've . . ."

"And they've got folks who got money and hang around with each other all the time—that's why." Melody Bolton finished Paula's little speech for her.

The only thing Paula Liven liked more than running everything was talking. When Melody cut her off, it really ticked her.

"Listen here, young lady . . ." Her fake eyelashes didn't flutter. Her drippy-sweet voice was a snarl. ". . . the fact that your mother's a barmaid had absolutely nothing to do with our decision. Our choice of players was . . . was strictly . . ."

"Your kids and their pals and your friends' kids," Kathy Fields said.

Mrs. Liven sneered at her. Kathy was a stout girl, and even with Paula Liven glaring down like she'd found a bug she wanted to squash, Kathy didn't give an inch.

"It's not fair," I said. "Brandon and Nick are both better players than T.R. and George, yet T.R. and George get to be on the team because they're your daughter's buddies. It's not fair."

Jerry left the group and walked off.

"If I was white, I bet they'd let me play," I heard him complain. My brother followed his friend through the door.

Paula Liven jabbed her fists into her hips. (If she hadn't been so fat, she probably would have bruised her bones.) She squinted down at me.

"Justine Smith! If you say 'It's not fair' one more time . . ."

Mr. Queen grabbed her arm.

"Tell you what, kids." He tried to make that sneaky voice sound sincere. "It takes eighteen players to make a full roster. That's the rule and . . ."

"Is there a rule what says you gots to have a full roster?" Randy Black cut him off. "There's twenty-five of us who wanted to play." He squinted at the numbers he'd scrawled in the nap of the carpet. "Reckon we couldn't have two teams? Reckon one team with twelve and one team with thirteen? That way everybody'd get to play what wanted to."

Billy Queen kind of cringed. He didn't even look at Randy when he went on with his little speech. "Neither team would have enough subs if we did that. We were as fair as we could be in our decision—but there's only room for eighteen." Billy twisted the end of his thin mustache between his thumb and finger. "Now, if you kids can find some others who want to play . . . if you can get six or seven more, so you have enough for another team—then, shoot, I'll coach you myself."

"I'd just as soon not play," Brandon said. Then he followed Nick and Jerry outside.

Billy Queen's beady little eyes flashed white-hot. Before he could say anything, the rest of us turned and followed the others toward the door. Paula

Liven scurried over to where Randy had done his math in the nap of the carpet. She brushed the numbers away with her foot.

Just before I slammed the door, I remembered her threat. So, just loud enough for her to hear, I said:

"It's not fair!"

As we sat on the bicycle rack in front of the library, all the others agreed with me. Our parents didn't run with the big shots in town. They didn't have dinner with them or belong to the same social clubs. The seven of us didn't kiss up to the popular kids in school, and I wasn't about to start running around with Leslie Liven and her friends.

We couldn't change our parents. We either couldn't or wouldn't change ourselves. But for the life of me, I couldn't figure out what we *could* do.

"We could find some other kids like us," Randy Black said finally, like he was thinking out loud. "You know, the kids who don't belong. We could start our own team."

We all glanced at him. Kind of like ice cubes frozen in a tray, our eyes didn't move, they didn't blink. We simply stared.

Leave it to Randy, I thought to myself, to come up with the answer.

CHAPTER 2

Need Players for a

BRAN NEW SOCCER TEAM

If intrsted, please contack
Justine Smith or Jerry Tate

When I saw the sign taped to the wall in the sixth-grade wing at intermediate school, I went to find Randy Black. I knew he was the one who put it up. It *had to be* Randy, because along with misspelling half the words, the poster was sloppy and smudged.

I found him in Mr. Sweeney's math class. Randy was sitting in the back. He had his head down. His nose almost touched the book. He had his tongue stuck out the side of his mouth, working on a math problem.

I marched straight to his desk and slapped the poster down in front of him. He jumped. I glared at him.

"What's the idea of putting my name on this?" I demanded.

Randy gave me that dumb look of his and shrugged.

"Well, we agreed yesterday that we was gonna try and get enough kids to make a soccer team. I figured you and Jerry was the smartest ones in sixth grade, so I figured you was the ones people ought to talk to about joining up."

I put my fists on my hips.

"Did you ever think about asking me if it was all right to put my name on it?"

Randy shrugged.

"I thought a poster was a good idea." He smiled. "I didn't figure we could talk to everybody about joining the team. And maybe somebody we didn't talk to would see it. Did I think dumb?"

His eyes looked real sad. I glared at him a moment, then sighed.

"No," I said finally, "you weren't thinking dumb. It's just . . . well . . . if you're going to put my name on something, you could at least make it neat and *at least* spell soccer right."

Randy looked kind of sheepish.

"My spellin' ain't too hot, I guess. Should I do it again?"

I shook my head. "No. I'll take care of it."

He raised the tip of his pencil from the smudged math sheet he was working on.

"I done another one for fifth grade," he said, pointing toward the fifth-grade wing of the hall. "I put Nick's name on it. Reckon I ought to go get it?"

The tardy bell rang. I spun and headed for the door.

"No," I called over my shoulder, "Nick can take care of himself."

I started fighting my way through the crowd that was trying to beat Mr. Sweeney into math class. From behind me, I could hear Randy call, "Oh, Justine, what's four times eight?"

I didn't bother to answer. Wiggling my way through the mob at the door, I shot down the hall. I slid into the doorway of Mrs. Heisler's English class just as the bell stopped ringing.

My tennis shoes squeaked when I tried to stop. Mrs. Heisler glanced up. Then, still sliding, my shoes hit something on the floor. It was a rough spot or something. Whatever—my shoes quit sliding. They didn't move. They didn't budge an inch.

I *did!*

I guess I was running harder than I thought, trying not to be late for English. When my shoes stopped, I kept going. I couldn't catch myself. I couldn't get my balance. Suddenly, I kind of pitched forward. I threw my arms out to keep from landing on my face. My books went flying toward the chalkboard. I went flying toward Mrs. Heisler's desk.

I slid halfway across the room on my stomach. When I finally stopped, the whole class burst out laughing. I glanced up. Mrs. Heisler leaned over her desk. She looked down at me over the tops of her little, gold-rimmed glasses.

"Nice of you to join us, Miss Smith," she said politely. "Don't you think you'd be more comfortable in a chair, though?"

Everybody roared again. I could feel the heat in my cheeks and ears. I'd never been so embarrassed in my whole life.

I struggled to my feet, with as much grace and dignity as I could muster, and got my books. The only one in the whole room who wasn't pointing or laughing at me was Oscar Dodd. Like always, he had his long, skinny nose stuck in a book. He had no idea that anything was going on. The rest of the class kept snickering and giggling.

"Quiet!" Mrs. Heisler barked, turning back to the chalkboard.

I hurried to my desk and sat down.

Everyone was still looking at me. Their hushed

giggles were a dull roar in my ears. I wanted to crawl inside the desk. I wanted to die.

"You come into a classroom the same way you play soccer," the voice behind me snipped. "No wonder you weren't picked for the team."

I recognized the voice. It was Leslie Liven's.

The plastic lunchroom chair was hard. Melody wiped the milk mustache from her upper lip with a napkin. "If Mrs. Heisler hadn't peeked over the top of those gold-rimmed glasses," I said, "I would have turned around and punched Leslie." I bit down on my milk straw so hard that my jaws hurt. "I would have jumped up and spit right in her eye." I squeezed the end of my fork. My carrots started vibrating like tall buildings in an earthquake. "I hate that Leslie Liven. Somehow, some way . . ."

Suddenly, a hand tapped my shoulder. I jumped when I saw the sleazy character who stood behind me in the lunchroom. He had long hair. It was dirty-looking, like it hadn't been washed in a couple of weeks. He wore a leather jacket with some kind of patch on it. He smelled kind of smoky and dirty, too. His face looked like a sixth grader, but the rest of him looked like some teenager out of a 1950s James Dean movie on late night TV.

"You that Justine Smith girl?"

I made a gulping sound as I swallowed the chunk of roast beef in my mouth. I couldn't talk. I didn't really want to. At last, I nodded.

"You the one with the soccer team?"

Reluctantly, I nodded again.

He smiled. It was a sneaky smile—at least, it looked that way, because only one side of his mouth went up.

"My name's Dennis. Friends call me Buck. Just moved here last week. I wanna join up."

Melody draped her arm across the back of my neck, like she was trying to protect me. "We're just trying to see if any people are interested. If we have enough for a team . . . we'll . . . er, ah . . . we'll let you know."

She turned back to her tray. The sleaze-bag just stood there. Melody and I looked at each other out of the corners of our eyes. Finally, the guy pulled a pack of cigarettes from his pocket and disappeared out the door.

Melody and I both slumped at the same time, sighing so hard we made ripples in our milk.

"Who was that creep?" I gasped.

"Buck somebody." Melody shuddered. "Talk about sleazy. Creepy. We sure don't want a thug like that on our team."

We were in total agreement.

CHAPTER 3

After school, our group met in my backyard. I had dropped by the art room between first and second hour to redo the poster Randy had made a wreck of. I made a really neat poster and replaced the one Randy had messed up. But the only person who asked me if he could play was the sleaze-bag.

Melody had asked her friend, Carol Quinton. She really wasn't interested in soccer, but since she liked Melody, she told her she'd play—if we needed her.

Randy and Brandon had each asked about twenty guys. They came up with absolutely nobody. All the guys they talked to were busy either with track, tennis, or fall baseball, which started next week.

Randy looked disappointed.

"So, nobody at all came up and asked about the poster I done?"

Melody and I glanced at each other. We both had that same look in our eye. Neither one of us wanted to tell about the creepy kid at lunch. I looked back at Randy and shrugged.

"Sorry. Melody's friend Carol was the only one."

Randy turned to Nick.

"How about fifth grade? Anybody there wanna join us?"

Nick pulled a little spiral notepad from his pocket.

"Jerry and I asked Ruth Osako and Paco Santos. They both said they'd play—I think."

"What do you mean, you think?" Brandon asked.

Nick shrugged. "Well, Paco said he would, but his family moves a lot, so he might not be here very long. When I asked Ruth, I think she said yes, but I'm not sure. She's awful hard to understand."

"Yeah," Jerry agreed with him, "they just moved here from Japan. She hasn't mastered the English language yet. We asked them because soccer is really big in Japan. Paco's from Argentina. Everybody grows up playing soccer in Argentina. I bet he's great."

"No kiddin'," Brandon agreed. "Argentina's won the World Cup a bunch of times. Kids from Argentina are probably some of the best soccer players in the world."

Everybody seemed impressed. Everybody except Randy.

"How about the poster? Did anybody see the poster and ask about joining?"

Nick looked at Jerry, then back at his notepad. "Ah . . . er . . ." he stammered.

Jerry nudged him with an elbow. Nick put his notepad in his lap. He folded his arms. Jerry nudged him again.

"Oh, all right. Oscar Dodd asked Jerry about joining."

"Oscar Dodd???"

We all gasped.

"The Bookworm?" someone giggled.

"The Stork?" someone else shrieked. "He's in sixth grade. Why'd he ask Jerry?"

Jerry folded his arms, too.

"He asked Jerry because he was afraid Justine would make fun of him. That's why he came down to fifth grade. He was afraid you guys would call him names like 'Bookworm' or 'Stork.' Just like what you're doing."

That sort of shut everybody up.

"He's read a lot of books on soccer, and . . ." Jerry began.

"We need somebody who can *play* soccer," Brandon barged in, "not somebody who's just read about it."

"*And*," Jerry went on, almost yelling, "and he *wants* to play."

Brandon just shrugged.

"Anybody else?" Randy asked.

Nick clamped his lips together. They wrinkled and turned white. Finally, Jerry jabbed him again with his elbow.

"All right!" Nick growled. He looked back at the notepad. "Digger Zimmerman and Terri Jarman want to play."

I thought we had gasped loud when Nick told us about Oscar Dodd. But when he read Digger Zimmerman's and Terri Jarman's names, our gasp was more like a scream.

I guess I was the self-appointed peacemaker. It took some doing, but I finally got them quiet and back to at least discussing it.

"Maybe Digger," Brandon said, shaking his head. "I hate to, but . . ."

"Why not?" Melody jumped in. "I mean, we could make him take a bath before the games, and Justine or I could wash his clothes."

Her words had kind of an edge to them. I could tell she wasn't all that sincere.

Digger Zimmerman's first name was Paul. He had two older brothers and a little sister. Most of us didn't recognize the Zimmerman kids. Not from the front, at least. From the back, we knew them instantly.

As long as I could remember, the back end of one of the Zimmermans was always hanging out of a trash can someplace in town. If you saw a seat and a pair of legs dangling out of a Dumpster, they were bound to belong to a Zimmerman. Sometimes we'd see a scruffy-looking kid in dirty clothes, pushing a shopping cart full of junk down the street.

Digger Zimmerman's dad was the local junkman. We had garbage collectors who worked for the city. The Zimmermans knew the schedules and tried to beat the city workers to the *best* junk. Anything that could be fixed, polished, repaired, or cleaned up, the Zimmerman kids dragged home to their little white frame house.

Digger's yard was probably one of the few in town that was bigger than ours, but there was hardly anyplace to play. There were refrigerators, washing machines, dryers, scrap iron, boxes—everything you could imagine cluttering it up. I guess the Zimmermans kept the smaller stuff in the house.

Digger made good grades. He was nice to people and polite at school. Only, he didn't have many friends.

Usually, you could smell the Zimmermans before you ever saw them. Getting stuck next to one of them in class was a disaster—especially in late spring when the air conditioners weren't on. Though Digger usually wore clean clothes, a kind of aroma followed him. I guess it came from all the trash cans where he spent so much of his time.

Whatever the reason, we agreed that we could tolerate the smell—*if* Digger could play soccer. (You can put up with a lot when you're trying to get a team together.)

Terri Jarman was a different matter.

"Maybe Digger," Brandon repeated, "but no way on the Jarman girl. I mean, at Thanksgiving she caught Hal Sparks on the way home from school and beat the tar out of him. He's the toughest guy in sixth grade, and she's only a fifth grader—she's a girl, too." He shook his head. "Just beat ol' Hal to a pulp. No way on Jarman."

"Hal Sparks *used to be* the toughest guy in sixth grade," Melody added. "Since that little Jarman kid got through with him, he kind of avoids people now. You don't really see much of him. But I think Brandon's right—no way on Terri Jarman."

"Why not?" Nick insisted. "I mean . . ."

"I heard her older brother is in the pen," Brandon interrupted.

"Didn't he try to rob a bank in Oregon or something?" Randy asked.

We all nodded, then shrugged. We'd heard something about him, but nobody was sure of the details.

"Thomas, the middle one," Melody said, "he's in the Army or Navy, or something."

"Yeah," Jerry agreed. "But Danny, the one just older than Terri—he's in Juvenile Hall."

"No, he's not," Nick argued. "They let him out about Christmastime."

"No, they sent him back." Jerry shook his head. "But just because Terri's brother is in jail doesn't mean that she's . . ."

"I think we ought to let her play," Kathy Fields interrupted, finally getting into the conversation. "With Terri on our team, nobody's gonna mess with us. They do, we'll just sic Terri on them."

"She's fast, too," Nick said. "When she chased Hal home from school last year, she caught him a block from the playground. His legs are almost as long as Brandon's, but she ran him down in nothing flat."

I nodded, remembering the fight—well, it wasn't much of a fight.

"But if Terri's hitting people all the time, she'll get red-carded and thrown out. She's not going to help our team much if she keeps getting thrown out of games for fighting."

Brandon was quick to agree with me. So was Melody.

"Let's vote on it," I said finally. "How many want Terri Jarman, raise your hand."

Nick, Jerry, and Kathy raised their hands.

"How many don't want her?"

Melody, Brandon, and I raised our hands.

It was a tie. We all stopped and looked at Randy. He was a little slower than the rest of us, and it took him time to work things out.

"What do you think, Randy?" I urged.

Randy kind of smiled at me. He frowned again, thinking. Finally, he gave a sheepish smile.

"How many players we got?"

We all watched as Nick tapped his pencil beside each name on his little spiral pad. Then he pointed his pencil to each of us, in turn.

"Counting us, and not counting Terri . . . Let's see . . ." He counted again. "Twelve, without Terri."

Randy looked down like he was counting his fingers.

"Twelve. That would give us one sub, if everybody shows up. Somebody get sick or hurt, there ain't nobody left." He shrugged. "I figure, we let anybody who wants to play—play."

CHAPTER 4

I was beginning to wonder about Randy. If he was really the dumbest guy in class, how did he keep coming up with all the right answers?

I didn't have long to think about it, though. As soon as we decided to let everyone play who wanted to play, we had to figure out who we could get to be our coach.

Billy Queen, even though he had volunteered, was *out*. We all agreed we'd rather not have a coach than have him. So we decided to go home and ask our folks if they would coach us. Then, before we left, we decided to talk to the other kids at school tomorrow, and see if one of their dads might.

That was mainly because of Paco Santos. We figured that since he was from Argentina, his dad would be the best choice for coach.

* * *

Jerry Tate was the last one to get to my house after school. He plopped down next to Carol Quinton, completing the circle where we sat in the side yard. "Dad work late at the factory," Paco said. "We in school, he sleep and he go work when we get out."

"How about your dad, Carol?" I cocked an eyebrow.

Carol Quinton shook her head. "He's tired when he gets home. Besides, he says he knows as much about soccer as I do—that means, absolutely nothing."

We looked at the next person in our circle. Melody looked down at her lap, and we moved on to Kathy. She just shook her head.

"My dad's too busy fixing up stuff," Digger said.

Ruth was next. She didn't know what we were talking about, so she just smiled. Brandon's, Jerry's, Randy's and Oscar Dodd's dads all worked and didn't know about soccer, and Terri Jarman just sneered at us when we asked. That left Nick and me.

"Your dad doesn't have a real job," Brandon said. "How about him coaching us?"

Nick and I looked at each other. Daddy had always been real sensitive about people saying he didn't have a "real job." Mama used to tease him and say stuff like, "All you do is sit around and draw pictures or chip away at chunks of rock." She quit, though, because even teasing hurt his feelings.

"Just because Dad doesn't go to an office or have regular hours, doesn't mean he doesn't have a real job." Nick's words sounded just like the speech Daddy used to give us. "He's an artist. He works hard and it takes him a lot of time to do stuff."

"Besides that," I helped my brother out, "he's gone a lot. He has to fly to New York and San Francisco and places like that. Lots of times, he'd be gone when we needed him for games or something."

Nick looked at me. He seemed a little guilty.

"Yeah, and on top of that, Daddy's not much of an athlete. He could probably paint a picture on a soccer ball, but I doubt that he'd know how to kick one."

He kind of giggled. I just looked at him.

"We'll just coach ourselves," Brandon announced. It took him forever to unfold those long legs and get to his feet. "I know the rules and how to play. Justine's good, too. We'll be captains and choose up sides, then we'll start playing."

I wasn't crazy about the idea, but while Nick ran inside after his soccer ball, we chose up teams and went to the side yard.

Our side yard wasn't half as big as a soccer field, but with six on one team and seven on the other— and since this wasn't really a game—it seemed like the best place to play. The hedge next to the house, on the west side, and the fence on the east, would be out-of-bounds. Nick brought four little strips of cloth from the house. He tied them to the two center poles at the north and south ends of the yard.

"If the ball hits the fence between the poles, it's a goal," he announced.

We put the ball in the middle of the yard. Melody kicked off. She passed it to me and I set it downfield as she sprinted for it.

My mouth fell open when Paco Santos scooped it up in his arms and started running toward our goal line. He would have made it clear to the other end of the yard if Terri Jarman hadn't tackled him. She plowed into him from the side. She wrapped her arms around him, knocked the ball out of his hands, and left him flat on his back.

Nick went running over to kick the ball back into play. Brandon, Melody, and I just stood there, our mouths open, and looked at each other.

"We got the only kid from Argentina who never played soccer," Brandon sighed.

Nick passed the ball to Jerry, but before Jerry could dribble it, Digger Zimmerman grabbed him around the waist and tried to pull him down. Oscar Dodd looked confused—like he'd read somewhere that soccer was a little different from football, and you weren't supposed to grab people. Terri Jarman picked up the ball and ran for the goal. Ruth Osako and Carol Quinton just stood there and sort of smiled.

"Maybe we need to go over the rules, first," Brandon said with a frown.

"Your mom still have the whistle she used for second-grade recess?" Melody asked.

I nodded. "Think we're gonna need it?"

Melody's eyes rolled in her head. "No kiddin'!"

Brandon and Melody were explaining the rules to the others when I came back outside with Mama's playground whistle.

". . . and you can't grab 'em, Terri," Brandon added.

"What if they grab me?" she snarled. "I don't like nobody grabbin' me."

He shook his head. "You can't use your hands! Digger?" he turned to him, noticing the angry glare on Terri's face. "You can't use your hands either. Can't grab people. Paco? Got to use your feet. You have to kick the ball. No picking the thing up off the ground."

Both boys nodded.

We placed the ball in the middle of the field and tried again.

CHAPTER 5

"Please, Mama," I begged, "I blew that whistle till I was blue in the face. They just won't listen to me. We've got to have somebody."

Mama took a bite of her salmon patty. "I'm sorry, dear. I don't know the rules. I don't know how to coach you. And even if I did, I spend *all day* with kids at school. I'm not going to spend my afternoons coaching a soccer team."

"But, Mama," Nick pleaded, "they don't know what they're doing. Oscar misses the ball every time he tries to kick it. Digger and Paco keep picking it up and running with it . . ."

"Ruth Osako doesn't even speak English," I added. "All she does is stand around and smile. Carol's just as bad. She hangs around with Ruth and won't even try to kick . . ."

". . . and Terri Jarman was doing better," Nick went on. "Then Brandon tried to kick the ball downfield, and it accidentally hit her in the chest. She grabbed it off the ground and plastered him right in the back with it. You ought to see the red spot . . ."

"She would have killed Brandon if Nick and Jerry hadn't grabbed her," I said. "We've been trying to practice for three days—and everybody's getting worse instead of better. Oscar stands around and thinks. Paco and Digger wrestle with each other. Ruth and Carol just smile, and Terri tries to kill people."

"Justine's got to have help, Mama. The guys won't listen to her—or Brandon, either one. We got to have a grown-up. Please?"

Mama glanced at the mashed potatoes on her fork. Her eyes crossed for just a second, then she looked back at Nick.

"I'm sorry."

Nick and I looked at each other. We propped our elbows on the table and rested our chins in our hands.

Daddy was busy, doodling on a paper napkin beside his plate. He quit for a moment. He put the end of the pencil in his mouth and kind of chewed on it. I didn't think he'd been listening, but he gave a little jerk and looked at Mama.

"How about Paul? Is he still in town?"

"Paul who?" Mama asked.

"Paul Reiner. You know . . . used to be the principal at your school?"

My first thought, when I heard Daddy say Paul Reiner, was Oh, boy! He'd be great! My eyes kind of flashed, and I smiled. The smile quickly disappeared and a frown tugged at the corners of my lips.

Paul Reiner had been a neat principal. He was fun and had a nice sense of humor. The kids in our primary school liked him, and they also minded him and did stuff when he told them to. He used to help us and do things that would get us excited about school and learning.

Then, about two years ago, his wife ran off with the preacher down at our church.

Mr. Reiner changed.

"Oh, Ben . . ." Mama gasped. "Not him!"

Daddy picked up his pencil and doodled on the napkin some more. Mama picked up another forkful of potatoes. Nick and I just sat there.

"Why not?" Daddy nibbled on the pencil again.

Mama gulped down the potatoes she had just stuck in her mouth.

"He's not the same. He's totally different from what he was like before . . . ah . . ." She glanced at Nick and me, like she wasn't sure what to say.

"Before his wife ran off with the preacher." Nick said it for her.

Mama's eyebrows went up. "Well . . . yes. Before his wife left. He's a . . . a . . ."

"A drunk."

Nick helped her out again.

Mama plopped her fork down on her plate. "He's not a drunk. At least, he wasn't. He's just had some problems adjusting . . . and . . . ah . . ."

"He's a drunk," Nick repeated. "Everybody in school knows about it, Mama. That's why they moved him over to Eastside Junior High. That's what they do with all the teachers nobody else wants. They move them over to that school, 'cause nobody over there cares."

Mama took a deep breath. She acted like she was going to say something, only she didn't. She just picked up her fork and went after her potatoes again.

"I just figured he might be a good coach," Daddy said. "Remember that Christmas party your school had at their house about six years ago? He had all sorts of trophies in that room." Daddy tapped his pencil on his napkin. "Wasn't he on the Olympic team when he was in college?"

"No," Mama mumbled over her mouthful of potatoes, "it wasn't the Olympics. It was some kind of exhibition team."

"Well, didn't the team travel all through Europe and China? Even Russia, didn't they?"

Mama put her fork down.

"I believe so. But that was way back when he was in college. It was also before . . . before . . ."

"Before his wife ran off with the preacher, and he turned into a drunk." Nick smiled.

Mama glared at him.

Nick kind of backed away from the table, like he figured she might take a swing at him or something.

"He knows more about soccer than anybody else in town," Daddy said softly. "He loved those kids when he was principal over there. It might be good for him to have something like a soccer team to work with. Might help him as much as the kids."

Mama just shook her head.

"I doubt that he'd consider it."

"Yeah," Nick added. "Besides, he probably couldn't even find the soccer field. The big kids say he carries around an ice chest full of Coors in his trunk. The minute the school bell rings, he runs out to the car, opens the trunk and . . ."

"That's enough, Nick!"

The way Mama said "that's enough, Nick" shut him up. Daddy looked at him, too—that kind of look out of the corner of his eye that said, "You've pushed far enough." Then Daddy smiled at Mama.

"Wouldn't hurt to ask him, would it?"

I scooted back from the table when Mama

slammed her fork down. She stormed into the other room. I could hear her pick up the phone. Dial. She came back in just a couple of minutes.

"He said, 'NO!' "

Brandon and I tried for another week. It was a total disaster. Terri kept getting mad at people and trying to fight them, Oscar finally tried to kick the ball, but just as he was bringing his leg back, Digger darted in and kicked it out of the way. Oscar fell down and told Digger he needed to use deodorant. Digger got his feelings hurt and went home. Melody tried to teach Ruth and Carol how to pass. They worked with her, but if we tried to scrimmage each other, they just stood around and smiled. And Terri Jarman gave Jerry a bloody nose, because they were both going for the ball, and he bumped into her.

Nick and Jerry were just as bad. They knew how to play, but when everybody else started running around and wrestling with one another, Jerry and Nick were right in there with them. I couldn't decide which I wanted more—to kill my brother or just give up on soccer altogether.

Then one day, right in the middle of our practice—if you could call it a practice—Brandon stopped and motioned me to the side.

"I was just thinking," he said. "We got to have somebody. You, Nick, Jerry, Melody, Randy, Kathy, me—most everybody on the team except Ruth and Paco—well, we all were in West School when Mr. Reiner was principal. Maybe if we went over and asked him, we'd have better luck than your mother did."

Melody had come over to join us. She agreed.

Mr. Reiner didn't live in the house. The lady who opened the door told us that his wife got the house and sold it to her after the divorce. She pointed to the little apartment above the garage.

"He lives up there now."

Brandon stopped at the bottom of the rickety steps.

"Wife runs off with the preacher, and she still gets the house." He shook his head. "Don't make sense, does it?"

Melody and I didn't answer. We followed Brandon up the stairs. We held tightly to the handrail, worried about the unpainted, rotten planks of wood that led to the apartment.

Brandon made a fist. He raised his hand, then hesitated. He took a deep breath and knocked.

CHAPTER 6

We had a team, now—if you could call the group we had a team.

Still, no coach.

Mr. Reiner always wore a jacket and tie when he was our principal. He was tall and slender and smiled a lot. The Saturday morning we went to see him, he met us at the door of his garage apartment in a pair of yellow shorts and no shirt. His tummy hung way out over the shorts. The elastic at the top kind of folded over under his fat belly.

Brandon told us later he had what his dad called a beer belly.

Mr. Reiner recognized us from West School. He excused himself and went to put on a shirt. We shoved some dirty clothes out of the way and sat down on the couch. Beer cans lined the counter in the kitchen and the coffee table in front of the couch. The smoke was so thick and the ashtray so full of dirty, gray ashes and cigarette butts, we could barely breathe.

We waited for Mr. Reiner to come back. Then we told him all about our team. He didn't seem impressed, so we told him what Daddy had said about him being so good at soccer and the only one in town who knew the game so well. He didn't seem impressed with that either.

Then we told him how Mrs. Liven and Mr. Queen had treated us, and how they just picked one team and wouldn't let us play on it. We told him how they made us feel like misfits and how we felt like nobody wanted us and how badly we needed a coach, because the other kids just wouldn't listen to Brandon or me, and Mr. Reiner said he was sorry. Then he said no.

No matter what we said, Mr. Reiner said no.

It was the next day, after Terri Jarman gave Digger Zimmerman a black eye, that Melody said, "I think I know how we can get Mr. Reiner to coach us."

"How?" I asked.

"Well, my mom told me that he used to come into the bar where she works. Only, lately he hasn't been coming. She said that he ran up this big bar tab, and the owner told the waitresses not to serve him any drinks until he paid it off."

"So," Brandon said, "along with being a drunk, he's broke, too."

Melody nodded. "Sounds like it."

Brandon put his hands on his hips.

"So, what does that have to do with him coaching us?"

Melody twisted a lock of her blond hair around her finger.

"Well, he likes to drink, and he doesn't have any money."

From where we stood on the sideline, I saw that look in Terri Jarman's eye.

"Nick!" I screamed. "You and Jerry get her! She's going after Digger again." Then I turned back to the conversation beside me. "You mean, if we offered him something he *really* wanted, he might reconsider being our coach?"

Melody smiled. She nodded her head way up, then way down.

"Right."

There were deep wrinkles in Brandon's brow when he stuck his face between us.

"You mean, we buy him beer in exchange for him coaching us?"

Melody and I both nodded.

Brandon shook his head. "You can't pay a coach. It says so in the rule book. I read it when you guys told me that Justine and me were gonna be the coach. It's illegal."

I smiled at him. "I read it, too. You can't pay a coach. But it doesn't say anything about providing him with refreshments. That's all we'd be doing."

"But how?" Brandon gasped.

Melody pointed her thumb toward her house. "I get an allowance. I got a bunch saved up for a new dress."

I pointed toward my house. "Mama and Daddy usually give Nick and me money, if we ask. I got some saved up, too. I bet, between the four of us, we could keep Mr. Reiner in beer for the rest of the fall season, anyway."

"No," Brandon shook his head. "I mean, how is anybody our age gonna get beer for him? We're in sixth grade, for gosh sakes!"

Melody and I had both been excited about the idea. Suddenly, our shoulders sagged.

"There's no way kids our age can get beer." Brandon's shoulders drooped, too.

Digger Zimmerman tugged at my sleeve. "I know where we can get beer."

Nick and Jerry were still struggling with Terri out in the middle of the field. I hadn't noticed when Digger escaped and ran to hide behind Melody, Brandon, and me.

He tugged my sleeve again. "I can get beer," he repeated.

Brandon looked suspicious. "Where?"

"My brothers find lots of beer and whiskey and stuff in the trash." He smiled. "People throw parties and make themselves sick. Then they throw the leftovers away. Either that or some lady gets mad at her husband for drinking too much and throws his beer out. Sometimes, you get a guy who's trying to quit. He throws it away himself. Only, you usually got to get to those places early in the morning, 'cause if you wait until evening, he'll change his mind and go back to dig it out of the trash himself."

Kathy Fields shoved her way in beside Melody.

"We'd be better off looking for beer," she said. "It takes guys longer to get drunk on beer than it does on whiskey. That way, we'd get more coaching time."

Brandon's eyebrows dipped so far down they almost touched his nose. "How do you know stuff like that?"

Kathy looked startled and then kind of turned red. Without an answer, she went to help Jerry and Nick hold Terri.

Melody folded her arms.

"You sure we can find beer?"

Digger looked smug. "Hey, we're talking trash here. When it comes to trash, Digger Zimmerman knows his business." He looked real cocky. "Trust me."

CHAPTER 7

I felt like a Zimmerman.

Here I was, Justine Smith—seat and legs dangling out of a Dumpster—digging around in the trash.

I shoved a pile of papers out of the way and looked around. Melody was holding my legs to keep me from falling completely in.

"Anything yet?" she called.

"Not yet."

I shoved a garbage bag aside. Still nothing.

It would break Mama's heart if she saw me. She was a teacher. Everybody in town knew her. Daddy was a famous artist—not that anybody in our town really paid much attention to him—but he was famous in other places. It would probably break his heart, too. I shoved a pile of newspapers aside.

I could just see the headlines.

**Daughter of Local Teacher and Famous Artist
Rescued from Dumpster by Emergency Unit**

I shuddered, trying to chase the thought from my
head. Melody tugged at my leg.

"Anything?"

"No."

"Let's try another Dumpster."

She helped pull me out. "Digger said we probably wouldn't find beer or whiskey and stuff behind
businesses, anyway. Let's walk on over a couple of
blocks to that residential neighborhood." Her nose
crinkled. "You stink!"

I *did!*

Especially my hand and arm. I tried to hold them
out to the side so I wouldn't have to smell the rotten, stale stench of old garbage. It didn't do any
good, because my shirt smelled, too.

When we got to the alley behind some houses,
Melody and I took turns digging in the trash cans.
At the end of the block, we hit the jackpot. Melody
came out of a Dumpster with five cans of beer, still
in the plastic holder. We worked the next block,
found nothing, and went to the alley behind the

Zimmerman house to see how the others had done.

The thirteen of us had found eighteen cans of beer. Only five of them were the same brand, but we figured that wouldn't make any difference.

Digger told us to be really quiet. Then he lifted a loose board in the fence, and we all crawled through. In the back corner of his yard, we found six stoves and eight refrigerators. All the refrigerators had the doors removed, except one.

"We'll use this for our storage bin," Digger said. "Dad's already stripped the coils and the motor off the thing and the seal and handle are gone from around the door. But it ought to work."

We gave Digger our cans, and he stacked them neatly on the shelves. Then he closed the door and propped a stick against it so it wouldn't open.

"What does your dad do with all of this stuff?" Randy asked.

"Well," Digger said, leading the way to my house and the soccer practice, "lots of it he fixes up to sell. The things that he can't repair, he gets the parts off of and sells them."

"Does he get lots of money for stuff?" Kathy wondered.

Digger shrugged. "I guess."

"What happens to it?" she wondered.

Digger stopped and sort of tilted his head to the

side. "What do you mean, 'What happens to it?' "

Kathy jabbed her thumb back toward his house.
"I mean, my mom and dad are on welfare. We
don't ever have any money. But . . . well . . . your
house don't look much better than ours, but your
dad must get lots of cash from selling all that stuff to
people. What happens to it? What do you guys
spend it on?"

Digger didn't look at her. He didn't look at any of
us. He just looked down at the ground. Then he
started tracing little circles in the dirt with the toe of
his tennis shoe.

"My daddy never got through school. He
dropped out when he was in eighth grade." He
made the circles smaller. "He's always been
ashamed of not knowing much or not ever being
able to get a good job. So . . . well . . ." Now he
wasn't drawing circles with his toe, he was sort of
kicking at a little hole in the dirt. "Anyway, it really
embarrasses him that he's so dumb, so he told all us
kids that we're going to college and we're gonna be
smart . . ." He smiled. ". . . or he'll kill us."

He kicked at the dirt one more time, then started
walking again.

"He spends some of the money on food and
clothes and stuff. Some he spends on soap." Digger sniffed the back of his hand. "We use a lot of

soap, but it's hard to get that trash can smell off you . . ."

I glanced at my own arm and looked down at the smelly smudges on my shirt.

". . . but most of the money," he went on, "most of it we send to Denny. He's in school down at the University of Texas. He's in medical school. Next year, he'll do his internship, then be a resident the following year and start making a little money.

"Denny and Dad will both pay for Jacob to go to school. He's gonna go to business college at Oklahoma University. Then, Jacob and Denny will help me through school, and when I get out, I'll help pay Tina's way through."

Nobody said anything. We just walked to my house and got the soccer ball out. We didn't play long. We'd spent so much time digging in trash cans, it was almost dark.

Brandon called me about nine. He'd talked to Mr. Reiner. He hadn't agreed to coach us, but he would come and take a look at our team on Saturday morning.

"How much?" I asked Brandon.

"One six-pack."

*   *   *

That night, I spent a long time in the bathtub, scrubbing and scrubbing. Still, the stink of old garbage lingered. I tried not to think about Digger and his family. I tried not to think about how kids at school—even me—had made fun of him because he smelled. I tried to sleep, but I couldn't.

CHAPTER 8

We didn't practice that week. We saved our energy for Saturday, so we could impress Mr. Reiner and convince him that we were worth his time and effort.

Mr. Reiner showed up thirty minutes late. He had told Brandon he would be there at ten. It was ten-thirty when he drove up. His eyes were as red as the stripes on the flag in front of school. He must have had a rough night. When he walked to the bench on the sideline of the soccer practice field, he kind of tilted to one side.

He plopped down on the bench like a glob of mortar plopping on a brick. Digger put the small ice chest at his feet. It was a blue Covy with a red top. Mr. Reiner opened the lid and peeked in. In the cooler were ice and six cans of beer, none with the same label.

"So what do you want us to do?" Brandon asked.

Mr. Reiner pulled a can from the ice chest. He popped the top. We kind of ducked and stepped away from the spray. Mr. Reiner took a magazine from under his arm. He put the beer between his pudgy thighs and opened the magazine in front of the can—sort of hiding it from view. Then he lit a cigarette.

"Do what you been doing." He blew a puff of smoke toward Brandon. "I'm just here to watch to-day. Just see if you got anything worth coaching."

As we picked sides in the middle of the field, Brandon and I told everyone—*one more time*—how important it was to do our best. We especially warned Terri not to lose her temper and go hitting anybody.

"We got to have a coach," I pleaded with them. "You guys won't listen to Brandon or me, so we got to have this guy."

Kathy glanced over her shoulder.

"He's sorry. He used to be a good principal when we were little. He's sorry, now. Why do we want him?"

Brandon put a hand on her shoulder. "Because nobody else would even think about being our coach. Nobody we asked would even take the time to come and look at us. Because nobody else wants us, that's why."

It was the worst practice—ever.

Nick and Jerry played goalie. Only, since the ball never got near them, they both came out of the goals and started playing. Carol and Ruth guarded each other, but if the ball came right to them, one would try to kick it. Mostly, they just stood around watching and smiling.

Digger and Randy played hard, but they kept running into each other. Oscar did better than usual, but when he tried to make a hard kick, he slipped and ended up flat on his back. Melody tried to head the ball and got a bloody nose, and even Brandon and I screwed up. I guess we were trying *too* hard to impress Mr. Reiner. Brandon kept running as fast as he could, and when he did that, he ended up tripping over those long legs of his and falling down. A couple of times, on high passes, I reached up *with my hand* and knocked the ball down.

I was trying too hard, I couldn't help it.

Terri did surprisingly well. Randy bumped into her a couple of times and so did Jerry. Terri kept her cool, though. Until . . .

She and Brandon were going for the same ball. They both kicked at the same time and cracked shins. From the POP I could tell it hurt. But instead of falling down and grabbing her leg, Terri started for Brandon. Nick moved in quick and caught her. But she called Brandon a bad name.

Brandon's shin must have hurt, too. He forgot himself and flipped her off.

Terri flattened Nick and took off after Brandon. If he hadn't had such long legs, Terri probably would have killed him.

So, while Terri was chasing Brandon around the field, and Nick and Jerry were chasing Terri, and Carol and Ruth were still smiling, I glanced at Mr. Reiner.

He had kept the magazine in front of his beer can all the time. But he never read the thing. He just watched us over the top of it and smoked one cigarette after another and drank his beer.

When I looked over, he was finishing the last can. He had his head tilted back so far to suck the last drop, I thought he was going to fall off the bench. He didn't. Instead, he set the can down, belched, and waddled toward his car.

I chased after him. The others who weren't running after Terri, or who weren't standing around smiling, followed.

He was reaching for the door handle when I caught up to him. I sort of jumped between him and his Subaru, pushing my seat against the door so he couldn't open it and leave.

"Well, Mr. Reiner," I panted, "what do you think? You gonna coach our team?"

He glared at me through those bloodshot eyes.

"*What team?* You ain't got a team."

"Yeah, we do," Randy insisted as he scooted beside me to lean against the car door, too. "There's thirteen of us. That's enough for a team, and we wanna play."

Mr. Reiner shook his head. For an instant, his bloodshot eyes seemed to float free inside their sockets.

"If I had something to coach, I might think about it. I mean, the free beer's worth a few minutes of my time. But you kids got nothin'."

Melody slipped in beside Randy.

"If we had a coach, we might be something," she said. "We don't know what we're doing. That's why we need somebody who can . . ."

"You're right about that," Mr. Reiner said. "More than half of you don't even know what a soccer ball is. More than half of you don't know what you're supposed to do with the thing. You can't decide whether to kick it, throw it, or bite it!"

"We could learn." Oscar tried to smile. "We really want to."

Mr. Reiner belched. When he did, the smell of the cigarettes and beer almost knocked me down. I held on to the car door. He looked around.

"Listen," he belched again, "I've had a lot of you in elementary school. You're good kids, but you're not, and probably never will be, a soccer team. I mean, even if you had the skills . . ." He shook his head. "Even with the skills, you couldn't make a team out of this bunch. You're wild. All you want to do is run around and play. You have no idea about the amount of work . . ."

"We're willing to work," Melody spoke up. "We'll do whatever it takes."

The smell of cigarettes and beer even came from Mr. Reiner's nose when he sighed.

Brandon and Terri came up, followed by Nick and Jerry. What my brother and his friend had done, or how they'd done it, I had no idea. But Brandon had his arm around Terri's shoulder. Terri only came up to Brandon's chest, but she had her arm around his waist. Both of them were smiling, like they were the best of friends.

"We're okay now," Brandon announced.

"Yeah." Terri tried to laugh. She didn't fake it very well. "I just got a little hot. I was really just playing. I wasn't really mad."

Mr. Reiner's eyes rolled.

I put my hand on his.

"Please. We can't have a team without you. We want to play. We have to have a coach."

Mr. Reiner started to say something. Then his lips clamped shut, and he shook his head.

"I'm sorry, Justine, I didn't see anything to coach."

Suddenly, Kathy was there.

"You were so hung over you couldn't see anything," she growled.

Melody pulled her away. Mr. Reiner kind of pushed me aside and clicked the door handle.

"Please," I begged. "We want to play. We'll work for you."

"Yeah," Digger said. "We'll keep bringing beer. One six-pack for each practice. Please?"

Mr. Reiner tried to pull the door open. I leaned against it as hard as I could. I could feel the tears well up at the bottom of my eyes.

"Please, Mr. Reiner," I almost screamed, "we want to play soccer. We want to have a team."

Suddenly, he quit pulling. He looked down at

me. His dark eyes seemed to look right inside me.

"Why?"

"Because . . ."

"Because, why?"

Those red, bloodshot eyes never blinked. All at once, I wasn't talking to some smelly drunk whose wife had run off with the preacher. I was talking to my old principal. I was talking to him, just like I used to in the lunchroom, when Leslie Liven would make me so mad I couldn't eat the food on my tray.

"Because we want to beat those guys." I swallowed the lump in my throat. "We want a team so we can play them and beat them!"

He held me by my shoulders—made me look at him when I tried to look away.

"Why?"

Now the tears weren't welling up in my eyes, they were beginning to trickle down my cheeks. I could feel the wet.

"Because of how they treat us. They treat us like dirt. They make us feel like we don't belong. They make us feel like we're not as good as them. And we are . . ."

I couldn't talk anymore. The tears rolled down my face. He gave my shoulders a little shake.

"Are you as good as they are?"

"Yes."

"How about Jerry. He's black. How about Digger? His dad collects garbage. He stinks. And Melody? Her mom's a barmaid. How about . . ."

"Yes! *Yes! Yes!!!*"

I screamed at him as loud as I could. The tears were streaming from my eyes so hard, I couldn't even see.

The others didn't say a word. They looked at their shoes or at the dirt. Through my tears, I could see Melody. She was crying, too.

"Yes," I whispered again, looking into his dark eyes. "We're every bit as good as they are. But they won't let us be. They make us feel like we don't belong. They make us feel like we're not even good enough to go to the same school. But we are, Mr. Reiner. We *do* belong. We're just as good as them. . . ."

My voice trailed off. I sobbed and couldn't catch my breath. I couldn't make myself stop crying.

Mr. Reiner stood there a long time. Finally, he got in his car and closed the door.

We stood around, still looking down at our shoes. Melody put her arm around me. I could see the little spots of water where the tears fell from my chin to the dry dust. Mr. Reiner started the engine.

None of us looked up. We heard the clunk sound when he put his Subaru in gear. He cleared his throat.

"All right." His voice was a whisper. We could

barely hear it above the hum of the engine. "But it's gonna cost you."

As the little car disappeared down the street, we squealed and laughed and jumped up and down and hugged each other. Even Ruth laughed, although I don't think she knew what she was laughing about. I cried and laughed, both at the same time.

We had a coach.

CHAPTER 9

Some coach.

We met again the following Saturday. We didn't practice a bit. We just sat around and listened while Mr. Reiner told us what it was going to "cost."

He smoked his cigarettes and drank the six-pack of beer we brought.

"First off, it'll cost you a six-pack of beer, each practice. We'll practice two hours every Saturday. We will do nothing but work on skills and learn the basics. You kids who think you already know the basics will learn them again. On Monday, Wednesday, and Friday afternoons, you will practice on your own. You'll run ten laps around the field while dribbling your soccer ball, before you work on anything else. I won't be there, but if I drive by on my way home from school and you're playing around or fighting, the deal's off. Agreed?"

"Agreed," we said in unison.

"If you miss a practice, you better have a good excuse. Terri?"

She jerked, looking up at him.

"Terri," he repeated, "for obvious reasons, you're now the team bouncer. The team and I will determine if someone has a good excuse for missing a practice. Got that, Terri? *We*, not you. If the person doesn't have a good reason, you have our permission to beat the tar out of him."

Everyone kind of gasped.

"Brandon, Randy, Nick, and Jerry . . ."

They looked up at him.

". . . if Terri misses practice without an excuse, you have my permission to beat the tar out of her." Under his breath he added, "Figure it'll take at least four of you."

Terri gave them one of her meanest looks. Then, after thinking that there *were* four of them and remembering she wasn't planning to miss practice anyway, she kind of relaxed and went back to listening to Mr. Reiner.

He cleared his throat.

"Rule two. You will do what I tell you. You don't have to like it, but you *will do it!*"

We nodded.

He was making notes on the magazine he used to hide his beer can. He looked down.

"One—come to practice or suffer the penalty. Two—do what I tell you. Three—" He turned back to us. "Everyone has to have a soccer ball and shin guards. Any problem there?"

Kathy rocked forward.

"My mom and dad won't give me any money for stuff," she said.

"I can usually find one or two in the trash," Digger smiled.

"If we can't find enough, we can get some money from our parents or out of our savings," I added.

Mr. Reiner nodded. "Okay. Rule three—everybody will bring a ball and wear shin guards to practice. Rule four—you have to make Cs or better to stay on the team."

"What about Randy?" I asked.

Mr. Reiner looked at him. He frowned, just like he did that first day. He tilted his head to the side, thinking.

"Randy?"

"Yes, sir?"

"Didn't you have glasses in third grade?"

Randy nodded.

"Why don't you have them on?"

"They done broke."

Mr. Reiner's eyes got tight. "And your dad didn't get you new ones?"

Randy looked down at his lap and shook his head.

"How about the speech and language therapy? When you got to fourth grade, did you ever do those tests that I told you about?"

Randy shook his head again.

"I reminded 'em, like you told me to. Only they said they were real busy and had a lot of guys to test. They said they'd get to me later."

"Did they?"

Again, Randy just shook his head.

Mr. Reiner slammed his magazine down on his leg. It made such a loud popping sound, I thought he broke something.

"Lazy, incompetent, lousy . . ." he snarled. Then he took a deep breath. He lit another cigarette and took another drink of his beer. "We'll see what we can do to help Randy. But, rule four still stands. You have to make Cs or better."

We all nodded.

He patted the magazine on his lap and took another drink of his beer before he looked at us.

"Rule five is a biggie," he said. "I don't want anybody to answer me now. Wait until next Saturday. Think it over. Talk to your parents. Think about what might come up that you'd rather do. Think about all the running and training and everything else I'm going to have you doing. Think about the misfits on your team. Think about every bad thing you can imagine. Then . . . if you stay on the team, you have to promise not to quit. For two years—nobody quits."

"If we quit, does Terri get to beat us up?" Oscar asked.

Mr. Reiner shook his head.

"No. No penalties. Nobody beats anybody up. You just have to promise not to quit."

Randy raised his hand like he was sitting in class. Mr. Reiner nodded at him.

"Do we have to sign our name in blood or something?"

"No. Some of you will be in seventh grade next year. That means we'll be playing against older kids, bigger kids. But all you have to do is . . . well, next Saturday, we'll sit in a circle, just like we're doing now. The ones of you who aren't here will have decided not to play. Those of you who show up, we'll join hands and *promise* me, the team, and ourselves—we won't quit."

We all agreed to think it over. Then we all went home.

*   *   *

The next Saturday, we sat in a circle and joined hands.

"There's one other thing you need to know about rule five," Mr. Reiner said. We raised our eyebrows.

"I am the most important person on this team. This team can't make it without me. So, therefore, I can't quit. No matter how bad things get, no matter how rotten, I'm still important. I'll make some mistakes, but no matter how bad they are or how miserable I feel about what I've done, I'm still a good person, and I can't quit." There was a funny kind of look on his face when he smiled. "Now everybody point at me."

He let go of our hands and pointed at himself. We all pointed at him, too.

Suddenly, he was glaring at us. His face was mean and angry-looking.

"No!" he barked. "I said point at *me*. Don't you guys know where *me* is?"

My nose crinkled up. I didn't know what he was talking about. Nick was the first to catch on. Slowly, he turned his hand around and pointed at himself. Mr. Reiner smiled at him. The rest of us pointed at ourselves, too.

Mr. Reiner seemed very proud.

"You can't forget where *me* is," he told us. "Now join hands. Repeat after me."

"I am the most important person on this team."

"I am the most important person on this team," we repeated.

"I make mistakes. I do dumb stuff, but I'm still a good person."

We repeated it.

"I care about me. I care about my team. I WILL NOT QUIT!"

"I WILL NOT QUIT!" echoed across the empty practice field.

We sat there for a long time, just holding hands and looking at each other. Then Mr. Reiner had us get our soccer balls and go to the center of the practice field. He had us sit on the ground and stretch our legs. We did sit-ups, then push-ups, then we stood up and stretched some more. After that he put some little orange traffic cones on the field. They were in a straight line, and for two solid hours, the only thing we did was try to dribble the ball in and out, between the cones.

It was boring.

Mr. Reiner finished his sixth can of beer. He leaned back as far as he could to suck the last drop out of the can, and fell off the bench. He landed flat on his back with his feet sticking up in the air.

The next Saturday, we spent two hours passing the ball back and forth. Mama dropped by after her grocery shopping to watch us for a time. While she was there, Mr. Reiner hid his beer can behind his magazine. But the second she left, Mr. Reiner spent the rest of the two hours guzzling his beer and puffing his cigarettes.

At least that Saturday he didn't fall off the bench.

The second week in September, the sleaze-bag caught Melody and me in the lunchroom. Just like the first time, he appeared out of nowhere and was suddenly standing behind us.

"You guys got a team yet?" he asked.

Melody and I looked at each other out of the corner of our eyes. He smiled politely.

"We're still working on it," Melody answered, "but not yet."

"We might not even be able to get a team to-gether," I lied. "Maybe next year."

His brow wrinkled, and he tilted his head to the

side. I turned back to my tray. He stood behind us for a long time. Finally he walked off.

I felt a little guilty about lying to him. But who wanted some guy on our soccer team who smoked and had greasy hair and wore a leather jacket?

CHAPTER 10

"I want him."

That's what Coach Reiner told me when I explained why Melody and I had lied to the sleaze-bag.

The whole team clumped around the bench where Mr. Reiner sat drinking beer and smoking cigarettes. Ruth gave a little cough and fanned the smoke away from her face.

The sleaze-bag stood near the center of the field. He folded his arms and kind of rocked back and forth from one foot to the other as he waited.

Somehow, he had heard that we had a team and were practicing on Saturday mornings. He showed up with his greasy hair, his leather jacket, and his tattered blue jeans. The only thing different was he had on tennis shoes instead of the sharp-toed leather ones he wore to school.

"He probably belongs to a motorcycle gang," Melody said. "I mean, look at that leather jacket with the patch and the emblem on the back."

We all glanced around.

"Yeah," I added, "and his hair looks like it's straight out of the fifties or something. Look at all that grease."

We kept staring at him.

Nick chuckled. "If he ever headed the ball, it'd probably be so slippery, we couldn't even kick it."

We all giggled.

The ice in the chest rattled when Mr. Reiner pulled out another can. He popped the top. The spray went toward Jerry and Nick. They dodged.

"In other words," Mr. Reiner took a big swig from the can, "he looks different from the rest of you, so you don't want him?"

We weren't giggling anymore. We were still smiling, but when we looked at the sleaze-bag, we didn't giggle.

"He smokes," I said. "Melody and I saw him behind the wall, near the Dumpsters."

"A smoker can't run too good," Melody helped me out. "They get winded too quick. At least that's what my mama says."

Mr. Reiner had the can to his lips again. He stopped and peeked at Melody over the top of it.

"He couldn't be in much worse shape than you guys. Half of you have to sit down after dribbling through the cones the second time."

"He looks creepy," Nick said.

"He looks like he thinks he's really cool," Brandon added. "Only he's so far out-of-date, he looks stupid instead."

"His name's Buck Rogers," Jerry giggled. "That's some cartoon character who had a spaceship or something. Maybe this guy just got off a spaceship. He looks like it."

Mr. Reiner flipped the can over his head. There was still beer in it. It went flying through the air, leaving a trail of white suds as it spun. It landed with a clunk behind the bench.

"Do you guys hear yourselves?" he snarled. "Do you hear what you're saying?"

We frowned and looked at him. He waved his hand toward the sleaze-bag.

"What you're telling me is that he doesn't look like you," Mr. Reiner whispered, so only we could hear him. "He doesn't dress like you. He doesn't wear his hair like you do. In other words, he's *different*. He doesn't belong."

A little shudder grabbed hold between my shoulder blades. Mr. Reiner didn't need to say anymore. We had treated the sleaze-bag just like Mr. Queen and Mrs. Liven had treated us. We left him out because he was different. He didn't belong. He was . . .

"Just like us," I whispered. (I didn't mean to say anything. It just sort of popped out.)

Mr. Reiner glanced at me. His bloodshot eyes were soft. Nobody said anything. We all turned toward the sleaze-bag—I mean the kid in the middle of the field. Mr. Reiner waved for him to come over.

Brandon was the first to greet him. He offered his hand, then the others came up and patted him on the back and shook his hand and told him how glad they were he wanted to join the team.

"That's enough," Mr. Reiner told us. "We've got to explain the rules to Buck, first. He may not even want to be part of our team."

When Mr. Reiner finished telling him the rules, Buck agreed to all of them except one.

"Dad belongs to this neat motorcycle gang out in California," he said.

"Told you so," Melody whispered in my ear.

"And if he comes through, he might want me to go back home with him. My dad's a really radical dude. So are the guys he rides with. I mean he's great. If he wants me to go with them . . ."

Mr. Reiner got to his feet. He made kind of a grunting sound when he got up.

"Think it over, Buck. Next week, if you show up, we have this little . . . well, ah . . . kind of ceremony we go through. Think about it for a week." Then louder, to all of us, he said, "All right, you guys. Back on the field."

After we finished our stretching, Mr. Reiner had us dribble through the cones. Then we practiced juggling.

That's where you bounce the ball off your foot or knee or head, without ever letting it touch the ground. I was getting a lot better at it. Sometimes I could bounce the ball five times without losing it.

The sleaze-bag—I mean Buck—was fantastic! How many times he juggled the ball, I don't know. But all of us stopped and watched. He swung his leg back and forth. He bounced the ball off the inside of his foot, then off the outside of his foot, then the inside. He bounced it with his knee, then his head, then started swinging his leg back and forth, bouncing it again on the inside, then the outside, then the inside of his foot.

The sleaze-bag—I mean Buck—could dribble the ball through the cones without even looking down.

He never had to stop and go back to set up one of the cones, because he never touched one, much less knocked it over.

Like I said, the sleaze-bag—I mean Buck—was a *fantastic* soccer player. Now I really felt guilty about having told him we didn't have a team.

We did nothing but practice during September. Mama stopped by to watch us after school a few times. It seemed to make Mr. Reiner tense, having a parent there, so Nick and I assured her we were fine and could practice better without her watching us. Brandon's dad stopped by once, while delivering flowers, and Oscar's parents watched us. Mr. Reiner always left his beer in the ice chest or hid it behind his magazine when grown-ups were around. He always seemed a bit more grumpy, too. I think Brandon and Oscar told their folks the same thing we'd told Mama. After that, we were pretty much left on our own. In October we practiced some more. It was the same in November. And, the last month of the fall soccer season, we practiced some more.

Brandon read an article in the paper about how Mrs. Liven's team won their division at the state games in Oklahoma City. He complained because we never played any games. Melody complained, too. So did Randy, Carol, Nick, Jerry—well, I guess all of us did.

Mr. Reiner said we'd play when we were ready. He also reminded us of rule number two: "Do what I say."

On Sunday afternoons, we raided trash cans. Digger told us the weekend, especially Sunday morning, was the best time to find booze in the trash. When the refrigerator in Digger's backyard was stacked clear to the top, we took a few weeks off.

The sleaze-bag—I mean Buck—helped Carol and Ruth and Paco with some of their skills. By the end of November, they were getting almost as good as the rest of us. Brandon and Oscar didn't fall down as much.

Buck even got a haircut and quit wearing that greasy stuff. He said it got in his eyes when he played, and it hurt. He looked kind of cute with his hair short and fluffy.

Then, the last Saturday of November, Coach Reiner really smashed us.

CHAPTER 11

"That's just the way it is," Mr. Reiner smiled. "Remember rule number two. You agreed to do what I told you."

"But what's it got to do with soccer?" Jerry asked the same thing all of us were wondering. "I mean, I can understand dribbling the soccer ball to school. I can understand going out on Monday, Wednesday, and Friday and dribbling it ten times around the field, weather permitting. I can understand practicing our juggling before we go to bed. But this stuff about spending the night with each other or doing homework together or just going to each other's house to eat . . . What's that got to do with soccer?"

"Yeah," we all nodded.

Mr. Reiner smiled. "You can't play soccer by yourself. You have to be a *team* before you can play.

You guys want to be a team, then you need to know each other."

He sat down and opened another can. Oscar and Buck dodged the spray.

"We've got three months of bad weather and snow and stuff before the spring season starts. Some of the teams you'll be playing have been together since kindergarten. The players know each other like a favorite book. They know where the other person's going to be on the field. They probably even know what each other had for breakfast.

"You guys have a lot of catching up to do. You don't know your team that well, but by April, I expect you to. I want you to know what food your teammates like, whether they sleep on a bed or on the couch, what their parents' names are and what their folks do for a living. You need to know whether your teammates get grounded or spanked, what their favorite TV show is and their favorite book. I want you to know each other so well you can even tell me when someone goes to the bathroom or whether he sleeps on his back or his side."

Kathy bit on her little finger. She rubbed at the little scratch over her eye. She told me she got it when she tripped on the stairs.

"But my mom and dad won't let me have people spend the night."

Mr. Reiner shrugged. "They'll let *you* spend the night at someone else's house. And I don't think they can object if someone comes over and spends an hour doing homework, then goes home." He nodded at Paco. "Paco's got too many brothers and sisters. There's no place to sleep at his house, so he can do the same. I'll be coming by your homes this winter, too. I'll visit with you and your parents and when. . ."

My eyes flashed wide. I guess some of the others reacted the same, because Mr. Reiner stopped.

"Don't worry." He smiled. "I'll wear my suit and tie. I'll even eat some breath mints before I come."

We relaxed a little.

Mr. Reiner reached in the ice chest and took out the last can of beer. He belched, but he didn't open it. Instead, he took it to his car.

"I'll see each of you before then," he called over his shoulder. "But our next practice will be April third. You better stay in shape, too. Spring season, we're not going to spend all our time practicing— we're gonna play!"

It wasn't nearly as bad as I thought. Nick was a to-tal pest. I guess all little brothers are. Sometimes I even hated him and told him I wished he were dead.

But when it was his turn to spend the night with Dennis Buck Rogers, I sure didn't want him to go.

I could just see him being kidnapped by some sleazy gang of motorcycle riders. They'd drag him off to California, and we'd never see him again.

Nick had a ball.

Buck lived with his grandmother and grandfather. Nick told me that Buck's father left him with them so he could ride around the country on his bike. The grandparents' house was nice. They were sweet people and fun to be around. Nick came home, stuffed like a toad. Buck's grandmother baked fresh bread and chocolate chip cookies and kept poking them down Nick until he thought he was going to explode. Buck had all these pictures of motorcycles and mountains and deserts and everything pinned on his wall. Even though Buck talked on and on about how great his father was, Nick still had a good time. He liked Buck, and especially his grandparents.

I was almost as scared when I had to spend the night with Terri. I figured her brother, who finally got out of Juvenile Hall, was going to slit my throat in my sleep—or maybe do something worse. I figured her parents were even more dangerous than him—to raise three boys and a girl who were as mean and tough as Terri.

Terri's mother did absolutely nothing. Her husband had died in a traffic accident when Terri was little, and the family lived off the insurance. Terri did all the cooking, the cleaning, the laundry—*everything*. Her mother sat in front of the TV. Her brother spent the night with a friend. When he left and said he was going to go rob a bank, Terri's mother didn't even look up. She never told her kids what to do. She never got after them or even told Terri what a good job she'd done with supper or anything. She just sat, like a zombie, staring with that blank look at the TV.

Terri was really sweet, though. We talked about school and boys and how boring Mr. Sweeney's math class was. (I could remember falling asleep a couple of times, last year, when I had him.) I helped her with the wash before I went home Saturday morning.

Ruth's dad was a doctor. Their house was clean and pretty. There was a lot of Japanese art all over the place. I left my shoes at the door, because Ruth said it was the proper, polite thing to do. Her dad spoke very good English. Her mother bowed and smiled a lot. Now I knew where Ruth got her smile.

Kathy's house was the worst. I never got to spend the night, and when I went over to do homework, Kathy told me that her dad was in a bad mood and wanted me to come back another day. As I was leaving, I could hear him screaming and yelling at Kathy's mom. He used really bad language and was loud and mean-sounding. It was almost the same the next time I went. Only, it was after I got there that he started shouting at Kathy's mom. She asked me to leave, early, and as I walked away, I could hear him screeching at Kathy.

I felt sorry for her.

For three months, we did homework at each other's houses. The boys spent the night with the boys and the girls spent the night with the girls. We talked. We played. We laughed. Oscar and Jerry spent a lot of time helping Randy with his homework. It was rough for him to make Cs.

Mr. Reiner was busy, too. He helped Randy's dad get him some glasses and came over to our school one day. Terri had been sent to the office for mouthing-off to her PE teacher during class. She said Mr. Reiner came into the office while she was there. She told us that he threw "a ring-tailed fit" at Principal Martin for not getting that testing stuff done on Randy. She told us that Mrs. Martin yelled back at him and said something about reporting him to the superintendent and the school board.

The next Monday, though, Randy started speech and language therapy classes.

Somebody found out that Paco really wasn't from Argentina. His family was from Mexico, and they weren't even supposed to be here. That's why they had to move so much. In fact, they were just about to move again, when somebody told Mr. Reiner about it. He went to Jerry's house and got Jerry's mom. She went down to the courthouse where she was a judge and drew up some kind of writ or paper or something. Anyway, Paco could stay here for another year. His dad could still be a carpenter at the factory, and they wouldn't have to move or hide like they had been.

Mr. Reiner did like he promised. The first time he came to our house, he had on a coat and tie. When I greeted him at the door, I smiled when I smelled the Certs on his breath. He visited with Mama and Daddy and had them sign some kind of form that gave their permission for Nick and me to play soccer. He also told them he'd need a copy of our birth certificates. He only smoked two cigarettes all the time he was there.

The second time he came, he ate dinner with us. He didn't grunt as loudly when he got up from the table as he did when he got up from the bench on the practice field. I thought he looked a little slimmer, too.

On April 3, I realized I was wrong. Maybe Mr. Reiner was a little slimmer, but his belly still hung out over his yellow shorts so far that it folded the elastic down at the top.

"Our first game's in three weeks," he announced. "The next two weeks, we'll practice. The third week, we'll scrimmage. I've got the cones set up. While you're dribbling through them, I'll call out something about your teammates. Without stopping your drills, you will shout the answer back to me. I want the answers short and loud. I'm gonna see just how well you know your teammates."

We trotted to the field, lined up, and started dribbling our soccer balls between the cones.

"Name of Oscar's dad?"

"Bart!" we all shouted back.

"Randy's dog?"

"Puddles!" We giggled.

"Buck's favorite food?"

"Chocolate chip cookies!"

"Justine's dad's job?"

"Artist."

"Brandon's father has a trophy room. What's his favorite trophy? Brandon can't answer."

Nobody answered.

"Featherweight boxing champion," Nick called finally. "United States Marine Corps."

My mouth dropped open. Brandon's dad had a flower shop. I never knew he was a marine—and a

boxer. I never broke stride, though. I kept dribbling the ball in and out of the cones.

"Digger's oldest brother?"

"Denny!"

"Occupation?"

"Doctor!"

"No," Jerry said, "he's an intern."

"Intern!"

"Right. Jerry's mom?"

"Tenicia!"

"Occupation?"

"Judge!"

"Melody's father?"

The balls rolled away from us. One knocked over
a cone. We all stood frozen. Slowly, we turned to
look at Mr. Reiner. Then we looked at Melody.

CHAPTER 12

"**M**elody's father?" Mr. Reiner repeated. Only this time he didn't shout it. He asked softly as he walked toward us. He didn't have a beer can in his hand. He didn't even have a cigarette.

None of us moved. Melody looked down at the ground.

Mr. Reiner came right up to her. He got so close, his fat beer belly blocked Melody's view of her tennis shoes.

"Melody's father," he said, "was named Daniel Winefield." I couldn't believe how soft his voice was. How gentle. "He was a law professor at the University of Illinois. Melody's mother loved him very much. He was handsome, smart, fun to be with." His voice was even less than a whisper now.

We were so quiet, we could hear every word. "Melody's mother didn't know he was married. He only told her *after* she found out she was pregnant with Melody." He cupped Melody's chin in his hand and forced her to look up at him. "Her mother made a mistake. She was lied to. She was cheated. She was alone and scared. She dropped out of law school and went to work so she could make enough money to raise her baby."

The tears rolled down Melody's cheeks and filled his hand. My eyes hurt, too. So did my heart.

Without even knowing it, we had gathered so close our shoulders were touching. Mr. Reiner turned to Jerry.

"Is Melody's mother a bad person?"

Jerry shook his head. "She's nice."

He turned to Brandon. "Is Melody a bad person?"

Brandon shook his head. "She's sweet. She's pretty and smart, too."

Then, to me. "Is it Melody's fault that her mother and father never got married?"

I shook my head and wiped the tear from the corner of my mouth.

Then, to Kathy.

"Was it her mother's fault?"

Kathy shook her head. "Not really," she sniffed.

Then, to Oscar.

"Was it Melody's fault?"

"No."

Then, to all of us, he asked, "Are Melody and her mom good people?"

"Yes!"

He held Melody back at arm's length. He made her look at him. He made her listen.

"Melody's mother made a mistake. We all make mistakes. If you read your Bible, even Moses and Jesus made mistakes. We're people—that's all. Melody's mom is a good, hardworking woman who loves her daughter. Melody is a bright, pretty young lady. She's a good soccer player, too."

"And a good friend," I sniffed.

"And a good friend," Mr. Reiner repeated. Then, his eyes grew tight. A tear rolled down his cheek. He looked at each of us, then back at Melody. Still holding her shoulders, he gave her a shake. It was so hard that the tears went flying from her chin.

"THEN WHY," his voice was a roar as he yelled at us, "then, why," he repeated, "is she standing here, leaking tears on my soccer field?"

Nobody could answer. Even some of the boys had tears in their eyes. We stood and stood and stood.

It was Randy who finally moved. He came up beside Melody and put his arm around her.

"She makes good grades," he told us. "But . . . well, I guess . . . she must be as dumb as I am. Why else would she let something that silly make her feel bad?" He gave a little shrug. "Least, it's good to know I ain't the only dumb one on the team." He smiled.

I couldn't tell whether the sound that came out of Melody was a laugh or a cry. But she reached out and hugged Randy. And he hugged her back.

Then we were all hugging and laughing and crying. We clumped together and held each other so tight we could barely breathe. I could feel the wet spot on top of my head where Mr. Reiner's cheek rested. I could feel his fat belly jerk and bounce. And, above me, I heard him whisper:

"Now we're a team."

CHAPTER 13

Being a team helped our insides. It didn't do much for our soccer.

Our first game, we played Paula Liven's team. They beat us 14–0.

It wasn't a pretty sight!

Most of the time, we played defense. Buck broke and dribbled downfield. He got a shot, but their goalie blocked it. Most of the time, we couldn't even get the ball to Buck. In fact, ninety percent of the game, we didn't get the ball across the half-line. Oscar fell down and so did Brandon. Ruth smiled and passed the ball to their team instead of ours. I got called for two handballs, since I kept reaching out for high passes, and Terri got a red card from the ref for giving Billy Queen's son, Bobby, a bloody nose.

We didn't say anything to Coach Reiner, but I think we were all happy that Terri got in one good shot at Bobby before they kicked her off the field. Bobby kept slide-tackling people. He knocked their feet out from under them or tried to hit them in the knee. The second time he did it to Terri, she popped him.

I guess Coach Reiner saw it coming. Nick was playing goalie for our team. Jerry had hold of Terri, but he couldn't hold her without Nick. By the time Nick got there, so did Coach Reiner.

Nick and Jerry had her under control, until the ref pulled the red card from his pocket. He stuck it in Terri's face and yelled at her to leave the field.

Terri went after the ref.

Like I said, Coach Reiner must have known what was coming. He was right there. He grabbed Terri and picked her up. He kind of carried her off the field, tucked under his arm like a football. She was cussing and kicking and screaming and yelling every step of the way.

We were a team, though.

Despite the fact that the other team laughed at us, and their fullbacks, who played in front of their own goal, scored two points, and we lost 14–0— despite all that, we didn't take it out on each other. Nobody yelled at anybody. None of us told our teammates what a lousy game they played or anything like that.

We just shook hands with the other team, like we were supposed to. When Coach came off the bench, he brought Terri with him, still dangling under his arm. After we were through shaking hands and lying to the other team about what a good game they played, we went back and sat down in a circle by Coach Reiner.

He sat on the bench. Terri was flopped across his lap. She'd quit fighting him, trying to get loose to beat up the ref. Instead, she propped her elbows on the bench and rested her chin in her hands while he talked to us.

"Not bad for your first game." He smiled.

We just looked at him.

"You've done well on your skills, but there's a lot of things you can only learn from playing games. I'll be honest with you. Chances are, you probably won't win one single game this season. You still want to play?"

Without even thinking about it, we all nodded.

Coach Reiner nodded back.

"Okay. See you Saturday morning."

We started to get up.

"Oh," he said, stopping us, "can everybody get a pair of old sunglasses?"

"Yes," we answered, wondering what we needed sunglasses for.

He didn't tell us.

He just glanced down at Terri, who was still plopped calmly across his lap.

"One more thing." He looked around until he spotted Digger. "Can you come up with a bigger ice chest."

"Sure." Digger nodded.

"Not more beer," Coach said. He glanced back down at Terri. "But we will need a bigger ice chest. I mean a *big* ice chest."

Digger shrugged. "No problem. People are always throwin' 'em out in the spring, when they buy new ones."

"Good. Remember—sunglasses and a big ice chest."

We were still wondering about the sunglasses and the ice chest when we got to Saturday morning practice.

We didn't wonder about the sunglasses for long. Coach Reiner took masking tape and wrapped it around the bottoms of each pair of glasses. That way, when we put them on, we could see in front of us, but we couldn't see our feet without leaning way over.

We had to do the cone drills without looking at the ball.

It was hard. I missed the ball a lot and had to go back and find it.

Then, Coach came up with a tag game. We started out at the goal. One person began dribbling his soccer ball out in the field. Coach Reiner counted five seconds, then another person would take off and try to tag the first person, while dribbling another ball. If the second person tagged the first—he won. If the guy with the head start could keep away from him—he won. If one of us lost the ball first—we lost.

At first it was impossible. If you looked down, watching the ball, you couldn't see where the other guy went. If you watched the other guy, you kept missing the ball and had to go back and get it.

It was still fun, though.

The next game, we lost 9–0. Terri didn't get to play, because if you get a red card you have to miss the next game.

It didn't seem like we played much better, and we still didn't know what the big ice chest was for.

We practiced. We worked on passes and dribbling with our sunglasses on. We worked on head-ing the ball and running sprints, up and down the field.

We played another game at El Reno. We lost 4–1. Buck got a breakaway and scored. It was great.

We also found out what the ice chest was for.

CHAPTER 14

We called our team the Misfits. It seemed like a good name for us. Jerry's dad, Mr. Tate, drove his van to our first out-of-town game. Part of the team rode in it. The rest of us rode in Randy's dad's camper. Some of the time, it didn't run so well, so Mr. Tate drove behind Randy's dad.

I rode with Melody, Ruth, Buck, and Brandon in the back of the camper. Randy and Oscar rode in the front with Randy's dad.

El Reno's team was all boys. Within the first ten minutes of the first half, they were ahead of us by 2–0. Their coach made their forwards go back to fullbacks and put their fullbacks up to forwards. Then, he started moving people in from his bench and letting kids play who usually didn't get to that much.

With their people playing positions they weren't used to, it made for a pretty good game.

Coach Reiner had Terri playing left halfback. That put her pretty close to him—on our bench's side and near the midfield. The first half, she did pretty well. She only cussed at a couple of guys and did it so softly that the ref didn't hear.

Ruth and Carol took turns playing right halfback, and since Coach was trying out Brandon as goalie, he put Nick at center halfback. (Coach usually played either Jerry or Nick close enough to Terri so they could get to her quickly.)

The El Reno kid who played right halfback against Terri was a tall, lanky Indian boy. He was fast and had good ball skills. Terri kept up with him pretty well until he'd run the ball outside. She'd get the angle on him and cut him off, then right as he got to the sideline, he'd put his foot on top of the ball. He'd stop it, push it back with his foot, spin around, and dribble past Terri.

I was sitting on the bench because Coach had put Melody in my left forward position. About the third time the Indian kid did the stop-and-reverse thing on Terri, she got ticked.

Coach Reiner was looking the other way, trying to get our fullbacks to move up and catch their forwards off side. He didn't see her clench her fist. He didn't see that look she gets in her eye right before she tears into somebody.

"Coach," I called softly.

He didn't hear me.

"Coach," I called louder.

He glanced at me. I pointed.

"Terri."

When he spotted the look in her eye and the way she was starting toward the lanky Indian kid, Coach Reiner's eyes flashed.

"Nick!"

Nick looked up. Without another word from Coach, he took off across the field to intercept Terri. He caught her around the waist, just before she got to the kid. She was dragging Nick down the field, and he was hanging onto her waist—but they were both close to our sideline. Coach Reiner stepped onto the field and got Terri.

When he did, the ref blew his whistle.

Both teams watched as Coach picked Terri up. Carrying her under his arm again like a football, he brought her back to the bench. Then, with his foot, he opened the ice chest.

Terri's blue eyes were hot as embers when he set her on top of all that ice. She tried to get up, but Coach just shoved her back down. This went on for a couple of minutes, until Terri decided he wasn't

going to let her get up. Pouting, she folded her arms
and sat there, glaring at Coach Reiner and the Indian kid, who stood on the field wondering what
was going on.

The ref came over. He kind of scratched his head.
He looked at Terri, sitting in the ice chest, then at
Coach, then back at Terri. Finally, he shrugged and
reached in his pocket.

"I musta missed whatever happened," he said,
"but I got to give you a yellow card for coming onto
the field."

Coach Reiner nodded. He shoved Terri back
down.

The ref flashed the yellow card. "No one on the
field but players," he called out. Then he gave the
other team a free kick from where Coach had pulled
Terri off the field.

At practice the following Saturday, Terri got mad
at Randy for kicking the ball and hitting her in the
face. He didn't mean to. It was a good kick. But
Terri went after him anyway.

Coach put her in the ice chest.

The next game, at home against Edmond, Terri
got another red card. I was so busy playing my position, I didn't see what happened. I did see her

jump in the air and catch the soccer ball. The guy who kicked it was still running toward her when she caught it. Terri drew back and threw it at him, hitting him right in the face. He doubled over and cupped his hands over his nose and mouth. I could see blood dripping between his fingers.

Terri was safely tucked under Coach Reiner's arm when the ref red-carded her. Coach didn't get her on ice quick enough that time.

She didn't get to play in the game against Deer Creek, because of the red card, but when we played the following game, Coach put her in as goalie. He said if she was going to keep grabbing the ball all the time and throwing it at people, instead of kicking it, he might as well put her there. Besides, we needed Brandon's long legs and speed out on the field. And Nick was a lot better at fullback than he was in the goal. He didn't like being goalie, either.

Terri was a great goalie. As little as she was, I never knew she could jump so high. I did know that she wasn't afraid of anything or anybody. It didn't surprise me at all to see her dive for a ball—snatch it right out from in front of someone's foot—or crash into somebody to get the ball away from him. It did surprise me that she could jump so well and knock shots away.

The thing that surprised all of us the most, though, was the day we played Lawton.

*   *   *

Lawton kept their starting forwards in for the whole game. It was hot, and they weren't easy on us like El Reno had been. They just ran the score up.

Coach Reiner pulled me out because I knocked the ball down a couple of times with my hands. It got me a yellow card, and I'd get a red card and miss the next game if I did it again.

About midway through the second half, Lawton scored goal number eleven on us. That's when I noticed Terri waving her hand.

"Coach," I called quickly, "Terri needs out."

"Goalie change!" Coach Reiner screamed when the ball finally went out-of-bounds.

Terri walked calmly toward us. At the sideline, she yanked her gloves off and flung them to the ground.

"You hurt?" Coach asked. "Sick?"

Terri shook her head.

"You're doing a super job, Terri," Coach Reiner said. "If you're not sick or hurt . . ."

Terri walked over and lifted the lid on the ice chest. She plopped down in the ice.

"They score one more goal on me," she growled, "I'm gonna kill somebody."

Coach Reiner dropped to one knee. He didn't say

anything to Terri, but his smile stretched clear across his face.

Terri stayed in the ice chest and pouted even after the game was over. When the whistle sounded to end the second half, our whole team and all our fans rushed over to her. They crowded around, patting her, hugging her, and telling her what a great game she'd played. Mostly, we told her how proud we were that she hadn't tried to kill somebody.

Terri's bottom lip stuck out. It looked almost purple. "I'm glad the spring season's just about over," she grumped. Then, with a little twinkle in her eye, she added, "This stuff keeps up much longer, I'm gonna have a frostbit butt."

Everybody broke up. Even Coach and the parents started laughing.

I guess it was downright confusing to the Lawton team. They ran the score up on us. They beat us 15–0 but instead of being upset, we were laughing our heads off.

We laughed and visited and pulled Terri out of the ice chest before the rest of her turned as purple as her lips. Then we stopped at Wendy's on the way home to eat. We laughed and talked some more.

We thought we laughed hard that day. It was nothing compared to the third game of the next soccer season.

CHAPTER 15

We ended the spring soccer season 12–0. Twelve teams out of the twelve teams that we played beat us. We didn't beat anybody. The whole spring, we only scored two goals—one was the breakaway that Buck got. The other was a penalty kick that I got to take.

Paula Liven's team, the Hot Shots, laughed at us. They laughed at the name of our team, and they laughed because we didn't play very well. Still, nobody even thought about quitting. I don't know why. The thought just never entered our minds. I liked playing, I liked my teammates, and it was fun. We got beat—so what?

In a way, I was glad the games were over for a while. Our beer stash was running low. What with practice on Saturday, church on Sunday morning, and a game on Sunday afternoon, there was no time to raid the trash cans. By Monday afternoon, there weren't many unopened beer cans to be found.

In fact, we took the last six-pack out of Digger's junk refrigerator the Saturday after school was out. It took us three weeks to get it stocked again.

The first thing Saturday morning, Coach Reiner told us he would be practicing with us three days a week. Digger asked him if we had to have beer for each practice.

Coach said no, only beer on Saturdays. The rest of the week was on him. He also mentioned that he'd noticed more parents coming to the games and would appreciate it if we'd discourage them from watching practice on Saturdays so he could at least drink his beer in peace.

"You guys have improved a hundred percent this year," he told us. "The reason you're getting beat is because you're outmanned. The other teams have a full roster—eighteen players. That gives them four more subs than you have. You got two choices—either add more people to our team or be in ten times better shape than the teams we play."

He also warned us that if we went the conditioning route, it was going to be hard. We would be sore and tired, because he would run us ragged all summer long.

We talked it over while he went for a beer and a cigarette. We decided that we didn't know anybody else who wanted to join our team of misfits—and, in a way, maybe we really didn't want anybody else to join.

"All right. You asked for it," he said. "Monday afternoon at five—sunglasses, shin guards, and balls."

We drilled. We passed and dribbled. We jogged from the practice field, clear across town to the hill by Parsons' Corner, and back again.

As we drilled and jogged, Coach Reiner called out the drills.

"Brandon's mother?"

"Tina!" we'd bark back.

"Buck's grandmother?"

"Helen."

"Carol's cat?"

"Boots!"

"Ruth's favorite food?"

"Spaghetti!"

After jogging, we went to the garage under Coach

Reiner's apartment. He'd told us that we would be playing under-14 next year. We'd be competing against mostly boys teams. By fifteen, boys were stronger, faster, and usually bigger than girls. If the girls wanted to hold their own against them, they had to build some muscle.

I never pictured myself lifting weights. But along with the drills and the running, that's what I did that summer. Bench presses, dead lifts, squats— you name it, we girls on the soccer team did it.

On Saturdays, Coach smoked and drank his beer. We divided into two teams and scrimmaged. I usually got stuck as goalie on one team; Terri was goalie on the other.

My "friends" decided that since I always swatted at the ball, or grabbed the thing, they might as well put me someplace where I could use my hands without getting called for it.

Some friends.

I wasn't nearly as good as Terri. But I got better by the time summer was over.

We all did.

We could dribble the ball without having to look down at it. Coach would blindfold us and have the others run around in a circle while we passed the ball—with nothing more to guide us than the sound of our teammates' voices. We got where we could pass the ball to each other without even looking. We grew stronger. We were faster. We got so we could run clear to Parsons' Corner and back again without breaking into a sweat. Even Terri improved. She only had to sit in the ice chest once every two weeks or so instead of every practice.

Our fall season started at home with El Reno. We won 4–1. I scored off a feed from Melody. Buck scored twice—once with a crossfield feed from me, and once on his own. Melody got a breakaway and dribbled downfield. She scored her goal without an assist.

The next week, we played Lawton. The final score was 2–0. They beat us, but not by as much as in the spring, when they'd won 15–0.

Our third game, we played at a little town just east of Oklahoma City called Chalk Hill. Their team was called the Hornets. They didn't try to beat us, they didn't even try to "sting" us—they tried to kill us.

We should have figured what kind of team they had before we ever got on the field. Right before the whistle, they gathered around and put their hands together in the center of their circle. Then they gave a cheer.

"BLOOD MAKES THE GRASS GROW—
KILL, KILL, KILL!"

Brandon's dad said it was a marine chant. He'd heard it before. Only he didn't think a soccer game was anyplace for something like that.

"After all, it's just a game."

To the Hornets, it wasn't "just a game." They played like it was a battle to the death. They slammed into us, tripped us, and grabbed our shirts when we'd break away and dribble around them.

Daddy said the ref came from Chalk Hill. It didn't take long to figure out what he meant. When the ball went out-of-bounds, it seemed like the Hornets always got it—no matter who kicked it. If one of their players knocked someone on our team down, there was no whistle. If one of their players tripped over his own big feet, the ref stopped play and gave them a free kick. Even Coach was getting a little irritated with the calls.

It was a rough, mean, nasty game.

Oscar Dodd got his knee hurt when one of their players slide-tackled him—a good five seconds *after* he'd passed the ball. Another player elbowed Jerry in the face, and he came off the field with a bloody nose.

By halftime, Coach Reiner was mad! As soon as the whistle blew, he stormed out on the field and started yelling at the ref for not controlling the game. He was mad because they were cheating and trying to hurt his kids instead of playing soccer. When the ref ignored him and just kept walking toward the far sideline, Coach Reiner got really riled. He suggested the ref get his whistle, his yellow card, and his head "out of the place where the sun don't shine" and use them to start calling a *fair* game!

Daddy and Mr. Tate finally went after him. They got him to the bench and tried to calm him down. He yanked open the ice chest. To our surprise, there wasn't any beer there. He grabbed a Diet Dr Pepper and popped the top. He upended the can and drank the whole thing without taking the can from his lips. Then he paced up and down the sideline, came back to the ice chest, and did the same with a Coke.

The ref stood around and visited with the Chalk Hill parents. They patted him on the back, smiled, and chatted like old friends.

"One more crooked call," Coach Reiner grumbled, "we're out of here. We'll forfeit before somebody gets really hurt." He lit another cigarette, not noticing the one he already had in his other hand.

Coach Reiner never got the chance to forfeit.

CHAPTER 16

Right before the second half started, I saw Ruth's dad pull her aside. I didn't pay much attention at the time. But I did notice that he stood very stiff and straight as he spoke to her. She bowed politely time and again.

When the whistle blew starting the second half, I noticed Ruth Osako wasn't smiling like usual. Instead, she was all over the place. She ran, she kicked the ball, she dribbled, she passed. If one of the larger boys on the Hornets' team slammed into her or jabbed his elbow in her back to knock her down, she'd scramble to her feet and tear after him.

It was downright amazing. She was all over that field. She put long-legged Brandon to shame, the way she moved.

The Hornets took a shot at our goal and missed.

The ball rolled down a steep bank and into some bushes at the bottom of the hill. While Terri went after it, I trotted over to talk to Ruth.

"What's goin' on? You've never played this hard before. I never knew you were that fast."

Ruth smiled just like she always did. Then her face turned a little red.

"Ruth not be much mean or rough when play." She glanced at the ground. "Ruth try to be sweet and nice. Try to make people like." She raised an eyebrow as if asking whether I understood her broken English or not. When I nodded, she smiled again.

"Papa say cannot be nice to these people. Papa kind of old-fashioned. He talk about Japan and talk about honor. He say they mean and nasty team, and if Ruth not play hard and mean, she dishonor self, her papa and mama—and bring most dishonor to team." Suddenly, the smile left her face. Her little, square jaw stuck out. Her eyes grew tight. "Ruth not dishonor team. Ruth not quit."

Ruth not quit. Justine not quit either. None of us did. It was like little, timid Ruth Osako was our inspiration. She was the Japanese version of an Oklahoma twister. She played so hard and fast and furious, all we could see was the cloud of dust she left behind.

Even Carol played better and harder than ever

before. She was following Ruth's lead and was right in the middle of the action.

Despite the rough and nasty play from the Chalk Hill team, we were ahead, 4–1. We were bruised, bloody, and hurt. But we were winning.

Then things started to happen.

We had the ball on their end of the field. One of the Hornets' forwards was standing about ten yards behind Nick at our end when their halfback got the ball and passed it to the forward. It was an obvious off side, but the ref didn't call it. Nick and Jerry took off after the guy, but he was too fast.

Coach Reiner lit another cigarette. Now he had three going, all at the same time.

At the last second, Terri made this flying leap. She grabbed the ball right at the guy's foot and wrapped herself around it.

He kicked the ball anyway. Then he looked down at her—stood there a second—and kicked Terri.

If it had been a friendly game, probably one of us would have cautioned their team about Terri. It wasn't a friendly game.

I think Terri had springs in her legs. One second, she was lying on the ground at this guy's feet. The next second, she was balled up on his head like a coon balled up on a hound.

(I knew how a raccoon looked, balled up on a

coonhound. Daddy once did a painting of one, for a western art show.)

Anyway, that's exactly what Terri looked like. She was wrapped around this guy's head. She had one leg over his shoulder and was kicking him in the stomach with the heel of her other foot. He was screaming and trying to get away. Terri bit, scratched, and slugged him so hard and fast, he didn't know which way to run even if he could have.

Nick and Jerry went after her. Only instead of running like they usually did, they just walked over.

Coach got there about the time Nick and Jerry did. He plucked her off the guy's head and tucked her under his arm. The guy from Chalk Hill was bloody and crying like a little baby. His coach helped him up. Then the ref rushed up to Coach and stuck a red card in Terri's face.

"What about the other kid?" Coach Reiner growled. "You gonna red-card him for kicking my goalie when she was down and had control of the ball?"

"No," the ref sneered, "it was a fair play."

Coach Reiner spit on his shoe. The ref showed Coach a yellow card.

Terri didn't even have to sit in the ice chest. Coach just put her on top of it and started pacing up and down the sideline.

Coach put me in as goalie. The ref gave the Hornets a penalty kick. There was nothing I could do. The score was 4–2.

About ten minutes later, they got a corner kick. It should have been our ball since one of their players kicked the ball over the end line—but the ref gave them the kick.

There was a big, fat gal on their team named Ginger. She took the shot. It was a good one, and I had to jump to knock the ball away. Only, I never got a chance to come back to the ground. While I was in the air, two of the Chalk Hill players slammed into me. The next thing I knew, I was sitting on the sideline with an ice pack on my head, and Nick was in the goal.

Terri was sitting next to me on her ice chest. Coach was still storming up and down the sideline, roaring at the ref.

Buck scored again, making it 5–2. On the following kickoff the Hornets passed the ball back to their halfbacks. Our team moved forward, and again fat Ginger and another one of their forwards got behind our fullbacks. And *again*, when they passed the ball to them, there was no whistle for off side.

Jerry and Randy took after Ginger and the guy, but they had too much of a head start on our fullbacks. It was a two-on-one breakaway and there was nothing Nick could do.

Ruth came out of nowhere. From the far end of the field, she got to them right before they reached the goal box. Just as the guy drew his foot back for the shot, she streaked in front of him and stole it.

Fat Ginger, instead of running after her to get the ball back, stuck her foot out and tripped Ruth.

Ruth went down in a cloud of dust. The ref looked at her. He had seen the whole thing. But when she bounced back up, he didn't blow the whistle. He just let the play continue.

"That's it," I heard Coach Reiner growl, "I'm gonna kill that sorry little . . ."

He stormed out onto the field. The ref saw him coming and blew the whistle. He had already yellow-carded him for spitting on his shoes. He reached for his red card. Coach kept marching— right for him.

"Coach Reiner."

I glanced over. Terri was still sitting on top of the ice chest.

"Coach?" she called again.

He didn't look back. He was almost halfway across the field when Terri yelled at the top of her lungs:

"Paul! PAUL REINER!!!"

Coach stopped. He looked back.

Terri stood beside her ice chest. Very calmly, she opened the lid and pointed down.

Coach Reiner looked mad.

Then he looked startled.

Then . . .

Well, it was the funniest look I've ever seen on a grown-up's face. It was a real sheepish look, like some little kid who'd been caught with his hand in the cookie jar.

And, just as obediently as some little scolded child, he trotted back to the sideline and sat down *in* the ice.

It was the most hilarious sight I've ever seen. Coach Reiner—his long legs dangling over the side and his round beer belly pouching over the top of his shorts—plopped there in Terri's ice chest.

We all started laughing. Melody's mother fell out of her chair. Daddy laughed until the tears came to his eyes. Nick and Randy and even Oscar rolled around on the ground. And Coach laughed at himself.

He laughed even harder when the ref came over and stuck the red card under his nose.

"Your team is disqualified. You forfeit the game for walking onto the field."

Coach tried to look serious—as serious as anyone his size can while sitting in an ice chest. His lips clamped together. Then he made a loud snorting sound and burst out laughing again.

"All right," the ref snarled, "you're disqualified from the next game, too."

He stuffed the card in Coach's pocket and marched off. We just laughed at him.

When Coach Reiner tried to get out of the ice chest and found out he was stuck, we laughed even harder. Coach kept kicking and struggling and finally tipped the ice chest over. He got loose, but in the process, he got drenched with the icy water. He commenced to squealing and giggling and leaping around. And before it was all over, all of us were either on the ground, holding our stomachs from laughing, or rolling around in tears.

We finished the fall soccer season at 9–4. The only teams who beat us were Paula Liven's bunch of Hot Shots and the team from Lawton. The other two games were the red-card forfeits to Chalk Hill and Norman, who we were scheduled to play after the Hornets.

When winter came, we practiced on Saturdays. We lifted weights in Mr. Reiner's garage. We ran. We spent the night with each other and did our homework together and even ate lunch together in the school lunchroom. On Sunday afternoons, we scavenged the trash cans for beer. And no one had the slightest thought of ever quitting the team.

Not until the spring. That's when things fell apart.

CHAPTER 17

The Wednesday afternoon before our first game on April 5, Kathy Fields came to practice late.

We usually didn't put on our taped sunglasses until Coach told us to. Kathy had hers on.

Most of the time, we said hi to Coach before we went onto the field, but Kathy went straight out.

Coach Reiner followed her. When he asked her why she was late, Kathy didn't answer. She turned away and tried to hide her face.

Coach made her turn around and look at him. Her lip was split and puffy. He made her take her glasses off. She had a black eye. It was swollen, too.

"What happened?"

She tried to smile.

"Nothing," she answered. "I was late for practice, and I fell down my stairs."

A chill raced up my back. I remembered the times she had the red cheek "from bumping into the door" and the little cut above her eye "from falling down the stairs."

"There aren't any stairs at Kathy's house," I said.

The words just popped out of me. I didn't mean for them to, but I'm glad they did.

"She doesn't have stairs," I repeated.

The team agreed. They'd been to Kathy's house, too, to do homework. They'd visited her and her mom while her dad sat in his chair in front of the TV, drinking whiskey and growling.

Without a word, Coach Reiner took Kathy's hand and marched her off the field. He made her get in his car. She didn't want to. She kept crying. Before he drove off, he asked Jerry if his mom was down at the courthouse today. When Jerry said yes, Coach asked if she was real busy. Then he said, "Never mind. It doesn't matter if she's busy or not."

The next day at school, we found out that Coach had taken Kathy to Jerry's mom. Judge Tate had talked to Kathy a long, long time before Kathy'd finally told her the truth about her dad. Then she and Coach had taken the police to Kathy's house. They'd arrested her dad. They put handcuffs on him and dragged him off in the police car.

On Sunday, Kathy didn't come to the game. Monday, Judge Tate had the police bring Mr. Fields to her court. She didn't fine him or send him to jail. Instead she said she would "rule" on the charges later. In the meanwhile, he, his wife, and Kathy had to go to a counselor twice a week. On Tuesday and Friday evenings, Mr. Fields had to attend Alcoholics Anonymous meetings down at the church.

Jerry said he'd heard his mom and dad talking that evening when they didn't think he was around. "Mom told him that she didn't pass sentence because if she did, Mr. Fields would probably move or at least try to sneak out of town with his family. She wanted them here so we could all keep an eye on Kathy. She also told Kathy's dad that if she ever heard from us that he was drunk or so much as yelled at his wife and kids . . . well . . ." Jerry took a deep breath. "She said she'd find a way to put him in jail until he was old and gray."

Mrs. Tate was a sweet lady. She was fun and had a great sense of humor. In her court, she was as tough as Jerry was on the soccer field. There was no messin' with her. I think Mr. Fields got the picture.

Kathy didn't come to practice at all the following week. But when she didn't show up Saturday morning, the whole team went over to her house.

She told us she was too ashamed and embarrassed

to even think about playing soccer. She didn't want to be on the team anymore, she didn't even want to leave the house.

The girls went to her room and put her soccer clothes on her. The boys helped us drag her to the soccer field.

"You can't quit," we all told her. "Rule five, remember. Nobody quits."

We almost beat Lawton on Sunday. Kathy scored the tying goal thirty seconds before the whistle. After a ten minute overtime, we were still tied 2–2. Terri did a great job defending on the shoot-out, but Melody was the only one on our team to get a shot past their goalie. They beat us 4–3.

I was sorry she was so embarrassed. I was sorry she was hurt. Mostly, I was glad that people knew about her dad so he'd quit hurting her and her mom.

The next Wednesday Buck was late for practice. When he came, he was riding on the back of a motorcycle. He came roaring up to the bench. Three other guys on motorcycles, with leather jackets and dingy, long hair and beards, pulled up beside them.

We were working on passing skills. We stopped our drill and went to see what was going on.

Buck was excited. There was a smile that

stretched clear across his face. There was also oil on his short hair. He had it slicked back.

"Coach Reiner, this is my dad, Jeb Rogers."

Jeb Rogers stayed on the motorcycle. He peeled his helmet off and nodded at Coach. Coach nodded back, not quite as polite. Jeb smiled. Two of his front teeth were missing.

"Him and his friends were just cruising through," Buck continued. "He's gonna take me back to live with him in California."

I was holding the soccer ball against my hip. It dropped to the ground and rolled away.

"You can't leave now, Buck," I gasped. "Not with the game tomorrow."

Buck glanced at me and ignored my little yelp. He turned back to Coach.

"I just wanted you to meet Dad and the guys before we left." He gave a little laugh. "I mean, these guys are really radical. They're cool. I just wanted you to meet them and . . ."

Coach Reiner folded his magazine and laid it on his lap. "What do your grandparents think about your leaving?"

Buck shrugged and kind of laughed again.

"Ah, you know what dweebs old folks are. They're fussin' at me to stay. They just don't know how much fun Dad is, how cool. They just don't understand . . ."

Coach was on his feet.

"What don't they understand? They don't understand that he'll take you to California, and after a couple of weeks or a couple of months, he'll get tired of you or bored and dump you on somebody, right?"

Buck took a step back. I could tell from the look on his face he didn't like what Coach said. Then he tried to smile. I guess he was too excited about his dad being in town to get mad.

"Nah, man, he wouldn't do that. We're going to go . . ."

"He's done it before." Coach leaned closer to him. Their noses almost touched. "You told me what a 'free spirit' he is, remember? You told me about his girlfriend that you lived with in California. You told me how she found another guy and got married, so you went back to live with your dad."

Coach Reiner's eyes scrunched tight. "How long did that last? Two weeks? So he brought you out here and dumped you with your grandparents. Then he came back to get you, and you spent two years living in dirty houses and hanging out with the 'gang.' Spent a lot of time on your own. Finally he brought you back here again." He jabbed a finger toward the guy on the cycle. "You think that jerk's cool. I'll tell you who's cool . . ."

Buck wasn't even trying to smile now. The louder Coach got, the farther he backed away.

". . . your grandparents, Ben and Helen—that's who's cool. They worked hard all their lives. They raised three kids—one's a lawyer in Seattle, the other finished college and has her own realty business in Oklahoma City, and one . . ." He jabbed a finger at the guy on the bike. ". . . and one never grew up. They screwed up on one out of three. They're old enough to retire, then they get a grandson dumped on them, because their own son isn't responsible enough to take care of him. They could be sitting back, taking life easy. Instead, Helen had to get a part-time job at a laundry and Ben had to start selling used cars again. They're the cool ones. They're the ones who've given up their own lives, just to take care of you. And what thanks do they get? You're gonna take off with that sorry . . ."

Suddenly, Buck wasn't backing away anymore. He was right up in Coach Reiner's face. He glared at him, his fist clenched at his side.

Jeb Rogers twisted the handlebar on his bike. The motor roared. I guess he couldn't hear what was going on over the puttering, gurgling sound it made while it idled. Now he was getting impatient. He revved the motor again.

"Come on, Buck," he called above the rumble of the motor, "let's move it, kid!"

Buck glared up at Coach Reiner. "You don't say

bad stuff about my dad. He's cool. He's the greatest dad that . . ."

"What's the holdup, Buck? Let's ride."

"If you think that creep is cool, you're a bigger fool than . . ."

Buck's fist was turning whiter by the second. Jeb Rogers revved his bike again. Coach Reiner's fist drew up at his side.

Things were getting way out of hand. Things were turning nasty, and they were turning nasty fast.

If Buck hit Coach, Coach would hit him back. Then the whole motorcycle gang (although there were only four) would pounce on him.

Somebody had to do something—quick. Somebody had to calm things down, say something, do something . . .

Without even thinking, I jumped between them. I sort of shoved my way in and looked up at Buck.

"You can't leave, Buck," I pleaded softly. "We got a game tomorrow. And . . . and . . . well, remember? Rule five? Nobody . . ."

It was the wrong thing to say.

CHAPTER 18

"Don't give me that stuff about rule five," Buck roared at me. Then he kind of shoved me aside. "Don't give me that junk about 'nobody quits'! It's just a bunch of words! Just a bunch of bull!" He stretched to his tiptoes so he could look Coach square in the eye. "Coach doesn't even believe it. It's just some stupid stuff he heard someplace— something he made up. It's nothin' but a lie!"

Buck was yelling above the roar from the motorcycles. Coach blinked and took a step back.

"Tell 'em what a lie it is, Coach! Tell 'em how you don't even believe it yourself."

Coach Reiner tilted his head to the side. His frown furrowed his brow.

"Tell 'em what?"

Buck's teeth clamped down so hard I could hear them grinding.

"Tell 'em how all this stuff is nothin' but a stinkin' lie. All that sittin' around in a circle and holding hands. All that promisin' our team and *ourselves* that we won't quit. All that junk about pointing to ourselves and *knowing where me is* and how *I* am the most important member of the team and how *I* won't quit the team—and how *I* won't quit, myself."

Suddenly Buck stopped yelling. His eyes seemed almost black as he glared into Coach Reiner's eyes. He didn't blink. I couldn't even see him breathe. Then, almost in a whisper, he said:

"If you really believed it—if it wasn't a lie—then why did *you* quit?"

Coach's head kind of popped back.

"I . . . I . . . didn't. I've been here every practice. I haven't missed a game. I . . ."

"I'm not talking soccer, Coach." Buck's voice was still barely a whisper. "I'm talkin' quitting. You quit."

Coach shook his head. "No. I didn't. I . . ."

Buck nodded.

"Yeah, you did. You quit. Three years ago when your wife ran off with that preacher. The team told me about it. They told me how you used to be a good principal. They told me how you used to be nice and fun. They told me how you cared about them and took care of them when they were little and going to your school.

"Then you quit. You quit being Paul Reiner. You turned into a fat drunk who smokes too much."

Coach Reiner stood frozen. Buck's words had knocked the air out of him. Maybe the words had reached clear inside and yanked his very soul out. He didn't blink. He just stood there.

VARROOM! VARROOM!

"Come on, Buck, let's go!"

Buck blinked. He looked down at the ground and shook his head.

"You quit, Coach. I can, too."

He turned and started to walk away. Coach didn't move. Jeb Rogers revved his engine. Buck hesitated. For just a second, he paused and looked back.

We didn't move. Coach didn't try to hide the tears that streamed down his cheeks. He didn't move either. He just stood there, looking at each of us.

Then he glanced down at the ground. With head bowed and shoulders slumped, he turned and walked to his car.

We watched the taillights disappear around the corner at the stop sign, two blocks away.

Buck hopped on the motorcycle behind his dad, and we watched them ride off.

We stood around for a long, long time. Finally, Nick picked up his soccer ball and tucked it under his arm.

"Looks like we're gonna have a short soccer season."

Then he headed home.

I was the last one to leave the practice field. I don't think I've ever felt so down or low in my whole life as when I tucked my soccer ball under my arm. It was like all my hopes and dreams were gone. I was empty. I was nothing—a nobody.

One last time, I glanced over my shoulder at the field. It hurt my insides. I shrugged.

Well, maybe that's how quitting is supposed to make a person feel.

CHAPTER 19

I thought I felt bad Wednesday afternoon, but it was nothing compared to the "bad" I felt when Leslie Liven caught me at my locker Thursday morning.

"Too bad about your coach quitting." Like her mother the day she told us we didn't make the team, Leslie Liven's voice was oozy-sweet as drippy syrup. "I hear your top scoring forward joined a motorcycle gang and left town." She fluttered her eyes. "What a shame."

I didn't say anything to her. I just stood there, looking over the top of my locker door.

Daddy always said: "You shouldn't kick somebody when they're down." It was an old-time expression that he used. I never knew what it meant, not until now.

I was down and out. There was no fight left in me, and with her drippy-sweet voice, Leslie Liven was kicking the snot out of me. For a second, I thought about crawling into my locker and closing the door.

When I didn't respond, Leslie gave a little laugh. "It wouldn't have mattered anyway. We've already beaten the Norman team. They were ranked number one. We beat Lawton, too." She fluffed her hair with a flip of her hand. "When you guys almost beat Lawton, it was really a surprise. Mom and Billy Queen hired a professional trainer from Dallas to work with us. He's getting us ready for the state games. I don't know why we were worried, though. You guys are just a bunch of losers." She forced her shoulders back. A prissy little smile wrinkled her lips and sort of shoved her nose up in the air. "We're going to win the state championship this year."

I ducked behind my locker door. I felt weak. Sick. I wanted to die.

"You wouldn't want to make a little bet on the state championship, would you?"

I was startled by a voice behind me. I wasn't nearly as startled as Leslie. When I peeked over my locker, her eyes were as big around as eggs frying in a skillet. Her mouth flopped open. I turned to see where the voice had come from and why she looked so shocked.

Buck Rogers and Brandon stood behind me.

Buck's hair wasn't slicked down with grease. It was fluffy and clean. He had on a crisp shirt instead of his leather jacket.

"Well, Leslie," he grinned, "you want to put some money on the game or are you just shooting your big mouth off."

"I . . . I thought . . ." Leslie stammered.

Brandon folded his arms. "You shouldn't try to think, Leslie." His voice was as drippy-sweet as hers had been. "Thinking's too hard on somebody like you."

"But . . . but . . ." Leslie cleared her throat. "Carl Perkins saw you leaving the soccer field on a motorcycle. He said it was your dad and you were going with him."

Buck nodded. "It was my dad, but I'm right here."

"And . . ." She made a gulping sound when she swallowed. ". . . and Jeffrey Plat's mom teaches at Eastside Junior High. She said Mr. Reiner left town."

Buck nodded again. "But he's coming back."

Leslie tried to look mean.

"We'll see about that." She spun and stomped off down the hall. "We'll just see about that," she repeated.

Brandon and Buck laughed.

I waited until she huffed around the corner at the side of the science lab. Then I leaped on the two boys behind me. I didn't think about being in the hall at school. I didn't think about how unladylike it might look to jump on two boys and wrap my arms around them and kiss them, on one cheek, then the other as hard and fast as I could.

I just did it.

They didn't shove me away. They didn't seem the least bit embarrassed that a goofy girl was kissing and hugging them in the middle of the hall. They just stood there, patting me on the shoulders until I stopped.

Buck told me that he felt bad about the way he talked to Coach Reiner. After he decided to stay with his grandparents, he went over to Coach's apartment to apologize.

"He was packing his car when I got there," Buck said.

"Running away?" I asked.

"That's what I thought," Buck admitted. "But he told me that I was right about him being a drunk. He said he'd known it for a long time, only he kept trying to deny it—kept lying to himself and pretending he really wasn't."

I bit at my bottom lip. "But why did he leave town?"

Buck smiled. "He said he was going to Michigan State University to see his old soccer coach. The guy's retired, but Coach said that the old man had taught him a lot. He said that maybe his old coach could help 'dry him out' and get him back on track. Jerry's dad is going to fill in for him until he gets back."

I tilted my head. Buck's eyes were soft and warm.

"How about you?" I smiled. "What made you decide to stay?"

"I . . ." Buck glanced down at the floor.

"Buck?"

He looked at me again and cleared his throat. He started to speak. His mouth opened, but no words came out. Then he held out a paper bag. I looked inside.

"Chocolate chip cookies?"

He shrugged. "Dad never could make chocolate chip cookies. Grandma's are great. Want one?"

I knew there was a lot more to it than cookies. Whatever made Buck stay, I could tell he wasn't ready to talk about it. It's just his way. So I took a cookie and went to class.

Jerry's dad wasn't a soccer coach. He was a piano teacher. It didn't matter. We were fired up. We had a team. Our coach was going to stop drinking and be a real coach. Everything was going right for a change.

We beat Yukon 4–1. The following week, we beat Noble 1–0.

Three teams were allowed to attend the state games. All we had to do was beat Norman on Sunday and we were in. That meant that even if Paula Liven's team, who played us the last game of the regular season, beat us, we still had a chance to play them again at state and win the championship.

Coach Reiner was supposed to be back by Sunday. With a coach—a real coach—we'd be ready. We were cool. We were tough. We were no longer a bunch of losers. We were winners.

CHAPTER 20

Even though Coach Reiner wasn't there for the start of the game on Sunday, we played like winners.

Norman was probably the best team we'd played. They had better skills than Lawton, who had beaten us earlier in the season. Still, we were leading by 2–0 at the half. We were winning. Until . . .

The second half had just started when Nick saw Coach Reiner's car.

"Here he comes!" Nick screamed.

Our whole team stopped in its tracks. We spotted his car coming up the street.

"Help!"

Terri's scream brought us back to the game. It was too late. One of their forwards had the ball and was headed for the goal. Before Nick and Jerry could get back, he shot. Lucky for us, the ball went wide of the goal. While Terri went after it, we headed toward our sideline to greet Coach.

Only, Coach didn't park behind *our* bench, like he always did. He drove right past. His car weaved back and forth as he circled the field, almost hitting a blue Datsun that belonged to one of the Norman parents, and slid to a stop behind the bleachers on the far side of the field.

Terri put the ball down on the chalk line, but she didn't take the goal kick. She was busy watching Coach Reiner's car. So were all the Norman players. Even the ref forgot there was a game going on.

Coach Reiner opened the car door. He didn't step out, he tumbled out. Clumped together like a herd of buffalo, we started across the field. Struggling, Coach finally got to his feet. He dusted himself off and staggered toward the Norman bench.

"He's drunk," Brandon gasped.

We had been rushing to greet him. About halfway across the field, we stopped.

Norman had seven subs lined up on their bench. Coach walked up beside one of them and patted him on the shoulder. Nervous, the kid jumped up and headed toward the bleachers where his parents were.

"Hey, you guys," Coach Reiner blurted out. He was loud and his speech was slurred. "You got new uniforms while I was gone. They look good on ya."

Nick was standing beside me in the center of the soccer field. "He's so drunk, he doesn't even know he's on the wrong side of the field. He's talking to the wrong team."

My shoulders sagged.

"Get away from those kids, you drunk!" one of their moms shouted.

"Somebody get this sot out of here," one of their fathers demanded.

Two men came from the Norman bleachers to get between Coach Reiner and their kids on the bench. We stood huddled together in disbelief. Finally, Buck broke from our group and ran to the sideline.

"Coach! What happened? Why'd you go and get drunk again?"

Coach Reiner turned his head, slowly trying to search out the person who was screaming at him. His eyes crossed, then uncrossed, then crossed again before he found Buck.

"Hey, Buck." He staggered toward him. "How you doin', Buck—how's my little Buckaroo?"

Buck's fists shook at his sides. "Why'd you get drunk again, Coach?"

"I ain't drunk. Just had one little beer." He took

a step toward Buck and almost fell. "Just one little drink."

"You promised, Coach!" Buck raged. "You said you were gonna find your old coach and dry out. It was a promise. . . ."

Coach Reiner laughed. "Yeah. Old Coach Parker. He was a good coach." He raised his hands. It was like a shrug only ten times more exaggerated and wild. "Old Coach Parker up and died on me. Died over a year ago. Just up and quit living." He frowned and leaned so far forward I thought he was going to tip over. "Say, how come you still got on your old uniform. Didn't they get you a new uniform, too?"

Jerry's and Randy's dads rushed past us and got Coach Reiner. As they helped him back to his car and loaded him in the backseat, the Norman parents kept saying stuff about getting that drunk off the field. They laughed and jeered at him. Mr. Tate sat in the backseat with Coach. Mr. Black got the keys and drove him off toward his apartment.

I was so embarrassed and ashamed, my heart dropped clear down to the bottom of my soccer shoes. I wanted to crawl under something and hide so no one would ever see me again.

The ref blew his whistle. "All right, you guys, we got a game to finish."

He marched both teams down the field and told

Terri to take the goal kick. While we were waiting, one of the Norman players nudged my elbow.

"That really your coach?"

I was too ashamed to answer.

He shrugged and laughed. "Man, I bet practices are really wild. He stay drunk like that all the time?"

My heart was already down in the bottom of my soccer shoes. Now, it just sort of drained out my cleats and into the dirt at my feet.

CHAPTER 21

"Hear you lost to Norman, 4–2."

Leslie Liven's voice echoed down the quiet hall Monday afternoon. I peeked over my locker door. She smiled.

"What a shame."

I didn't answer. I didn't even grunt at her. Leslie shrugged.

"When we beat you next Sunday, your soccer season is over. You're history." She almost laughed. "Your coach is history, too. That's too bad. He was the perfect coach for you. Talk about a bunch of losers, he was the biggest one of all."

She laughed out loud and walked off. A part of me wanted to tell her to drop dead. I was too tired, too beaten. I just went home.

*   *   *

"That's the sneakiest, most underhanded thing I ever heard of. It's not fair!" I could hear Daddy roaring before I even opened the front door. "It's just not right! We ought to do something about it. You get on the phone and I'll . . ."

He stopped yelling when I came in and plopped my books on the chair by the phone.

"What's going on?" I asked. "What's all the yelling?"

Mama shoved a piece of paper at me. I glanced at it. At the top, in big letters, it read:

SCHOOL BOARD AGENDA

I scanned the sheet. There was a line that said something about the budget. Another line mentioned new school buses. There was a sentence about somebody giving a report on the need for new football helmets. At the very bottom, by the number 7, the last thing on the agenda read:

"Paula Liven, Billy Queen, and Lee Orwell will speak to the board about a personnel problem at Eastside Junior High School."

I frowned and handed the sheet back to Mama. "So?"

Mama's nostrils flared. "So Paula and Billy are going to try and get Coach Reiner fired."

"It doesn't say that. It just says . . ."

"School board agendas never say what they really mean," Daddy snorted. "But that's exactly what they're doing. I bet every parent from their team will be there."

"How do you know that's what they're going to do?" I asked.

"They don't even have kids at Eastside," Daddy growled. "Why else would they go to the board?"

"So why are they trying to get Coach Reiner fired?"

Daddy gave me a disgusted look.

"Probably because of what he's done for you guys."

"What he's done for us!" The gasp that came from my throat was more like a squeak. "You mean embarrassing the devil out of us at the last game? You mean coming out on the field, staggering drunk and slobbering all over himself? You mean quitting, just when we needed him the most?" I spun around and stormed off to my room. "Yeah," I mumbled over my shoulder, "Coach Reiner has really set a good example for us kids. He's really done a lot for us."

I threw myself across my bed. I wanted to cry, but I never got the chance. I hardly bounced before Mama and Daddy came in.

Daddy folded his arms. His eyes were tight.

"That man has done a lot for you kids." His voice

was soft. His face wasn't. "Remember two years ago when you came crying to me that you didn't make the team? Remember how you said you kids were a bunch of misfits that nobody wanted? How you wanted me to coach you?"

I shrugged.

"Well," he went on, "Paul Reiner took you. He molded you into a team. A pretty good team, too."

"He made the school test Randy Black and get him in the remedial classes," Mama said. "He made Randy's father get him new glasses. And how about Melody?"

"And how about Kathy?" Daddy broke in. "How about getting her dad in counseling. And Paco and you and Nick . . ."

"What about me and Nick?" I snapped, interrupting him. "He didn't do anything for us."

"Oh, honey." Mama's eyes rolled. "You and Nick never stayed with anything until this soccer stuff. Remember the Nintendo game Nick *had to have.* He played with it twice, then it sat in the closet. And the piano lessons. How many practices before you quit? Three? Four? Then there was basketball and dance. You were always starting things but never staying with them. This is your second year to play soccer and . . ."

"But he's a drunk," I snarled. "He's a drunk and

. . . and . . . he quit on us." I laced my fingers behind my head and stared up at my bedroom ceiling. "He's just not worth it."

Suddenly, Daddy stood towering above me. His eyes were soft as he looked at me.

"I think he's worth it," Daddy whispered. "Coach Reiner went for five months and the strongest thing he drank was Diet Dr Pepper . . ."

I remembered the times Terri had sat in the ice chest and there was no beer in the thing. I remembered the times he paced up and down the sideline guzzling his pop.

". . . then something happened," Daddy went on, "and he slipped and started drinking again. He fell off the wagon. He got drunk. But I still think he's worth it."

"I do, too." Mama stood next to Daddy at the side of my bed. "He's having some hard times, but I think he's a good man." She smiled at Daddy. "I'll get on the phone and see if I can get some of the other parents to go with us to the school board meeting."

Daddy followed her. "You talk about kickin' a guy when he's down . . ." I heard him muttering as he trotted through the door, ". . . that's about as low as you can get."

I lay there, staring at the ceiling.

"Worth it," I said to a little silver speck that glistened at me from the plaster above. "Daddy's always using those old expressions—'kicking somebody when they're down; worth it.' What do they mean? Worth what? Coach Reiner's a drunk. What's he worth? Nothing! He's a loser, just like Leslie said."

Loser.

Loser!

The word pounded over and over inside my head. I grabbed my pillow and wrapped it over my face. I pressed the sides tight against my ears. It couldn't keep the word out: Loser!

CHAPTER 22

I waited until Mama and Daddy got off the phone and went to dress for the school board meeting. Then I took my turn. I called everyone on the team and asked if they could come over to my house.

Everybody I talked to said that their parents were going to the school board meeting. They said that their folks had told them *not* to leave the house while they were gone.

At seven Buck rang my doorbell. By seven-twenty our whole team was sitting in my living room. That's when I told them what we had to do.

* * *

The neon sign above the door flashed:

GREEN PARROT LOUNGE

"I still think you're nuts, Justine," Brandon growled. "You're totally out of your mind."

"Totally!" Buck echoed.

"Right," I nodded, agreeing with them. "Now open the door, and let's see if he's in here."

Brandon took a deep breath and opened the door. The smell of old smoke and stale alcohol swallowed fourteen kids when we flooded into the bar. The people, sitting around in booths and at tables, looked at us through clouded eyes. The bartender's mouth flopped open as we marched across the room like we owned the place.

"You seen Paul Reiner tonight?" Buck asked.

The bartender's forehead wrinkled.

"Who?"

"Paul Reiner," Nick said. "You know, tall guy. Big beer gut. Smokes too much. Paul Reiner."

The guy shook his head. Then he stopped drying the glass in his hand and flipped his towel at us.

"You kids get out of here. You can't come into a bar. Get, 'fore the cops find you in here."

We scanned the dark shadowy room one last time. Coach Reiner wasn't there, so we left and headed for the next bar.

"It's a stupid idea, Justine," Carol muttered as we rounded the corner. The No-No Bar and Grill was next on our list. "When we didn't find him at his apartment, we should have gone home."

Oscar moved up beside me. "Justine, even if we do find him, at the rate we're going it'll be too late to get him sobered up and down to the school board meeting. Let's go home."

I ignored him and kept marching.

Suddenly, Buck was in front of me. He stopped. When I tried to step around him, he moved to block me.

"What good's it gonna do, Justine? If we find him, if we get him sober, he'll just get drunk again. What's the use?"

When I jammed my fists on my hips, it hurt. I glared up at him.

"You remember the day Leslie Liven trapped me at my locker? I thought you had left town with your dad. I thought Coach had run off. I never felt so low in my whole life. Leslie knew it and she just kept kicking me. I was all alone. I was so beat I couldn't even say anything back to her. Then you and Brandon were there—just when I needed you."

Buck held up his hands. There was a confused frown on his face.

"So?"

I slipped around him and started again for the No-No Bar and Grill.

"So," I said over my shoulder, "nobody ought to have to feel that bad. That's the way Coach feels now. He's down and out. He's beat. He needs us—just like I needed you and Brandon that day Leslie was kicking me."

I stopped and wheeled to face the team. "And even if we can't find him or get him sober enough to go to the meeting, like I'd planned—he still *needs us!*"

Going into bars is a frightening way to spend an evening. It was especially scary for the girls—although I think it worried the boys as much as it did us. Bars are dark and scary. Some of the people who sat in the shadows were dark and scary, too.

Most people just stared at us. The smoke made us cough a couple of times. The bartenders yelled at us to leave. One big fat guy at a bar on Fifth Street tried to grab my arm when I walked past his table. "Let me buy you a drink, girlie," he'd slurred. Terri threatened to rip his arm off and beat him over the head with it. We pulled her away from the guy and kept looking for Coach.

* * *

"Have you seen Paul Reiner?" Buck asked again.

Just like the bartender in each place we'd been, the guy frowned.

"Who?"

"Paul Reiner," Nick answered. "Tall guy. Big beer gut. Smokes too much. Paul Reiner."

But this time, instead of shaking his head and running us off, the man sneered. "Yeah. Description sounds like the guy out back."

My eyebrows arched. "Out back?"

"Yeah," he answered. "Too loud and drunk for me to let him stay in here. I told him to get out and go sleep it off."

We rushed toward the back door of the bar.

Coach Reiner wasn't in his car sleeping it off. He never made it to the car. We found him passed out against a trash can behind the bar.

It wasn't a pretty sight.

Melody slapped him on the cheek a couple of times and shook him. He never blinked.

"He's out," she announced. "Cold as a mackerel."

He didn't wake up when Buck and Brandon dug around in his pockets, hunting for his keys. He didn't wake up when we dragged him to his car and stuffed him in the backseat. Brandon and Buck got in the front.

"Keys are in the switch," Buck announced. He reached for them, then stopped.

"Oh, no," he moaned, "it's a standard. Dad let me drive an automatic out in California a couple of times. But I don't know how to drive a standard shift."

Oscar Dodd opened the door. "I know how." He shoved Buck to the middle of the front seat and got behind the wheel. "Grandpa has a dairy farm. When we go to visit, on occasion he allows me to drive the truck in the pasture. I know how to operate the clutch . . . only . . . well, I'm not too adept at steering."

Brandon covered his eyes with his hands and shook his head.

"Great. Buck can drive but he can't use the clutch. Oscar knows how to work the clutch, but he can't drive. I want out!"

Buck took hold of the wheel. "You work the clutch, I'll steer."

"Great!" Brandon moaned again.

Oscar reached for the key but hesitated.

"I don't know." His hand shook. "If we get stopped . . . If the police apprehend us . . . my parents will never forgive me. They'll ground me until I'm forty."

Randy propped his elbow on the hood and smiled.

"Way I got it figured, we've been in almost every bar in town. Sooner or later our folks are gonna hear about it from somebody. It's ten o'clock. The board meeting's most likely over and our parents are home. We're gone instead of being in our houses like they told us to be. They can't find us, so they're already scared and mad. Way I see it, we're probably grounded for the rest of our lives, anyway. What difference does it make?"

Oscar started the engine. The rest of us stepped aside. The tires squealed. The car leaped forward. It made about six hopping, jarring bounces down the alley, then died.

"I thought you knew how to work the clutch?" we heard Buck complain.

"It's just a little different from my grandfather's truck. I'll get the hang of it."

There was a loud, shrill sound of metal grinding on metal. The car jumped and leaped again. It swerved from side to side as it bounced down the alley and onto the street. As it disappeared around the corner, we could hear Brandon's terrified scream:

"These guys are gonna kill me! I'm gonna die!"

CHAPTER 23

I was *sure* glad to see the car in the driveway when we trotted around the corner to Coach Reiner's apartment.

We were all glad that Buck and Oscar hadn't killed Brandon—or themselves.

Brandon, Buck, and Oscar had gotten Coach Reiner out of the car and were starting up the stairs. He was too heavy for them. They only got halfway, then gave up. Coach's head was on one step, the rest of him stretched out on the steps below. While the three boys were gasping for air, he was snoring—sleeping as soundly as a little baby in his crib.

It took all of us to lug him up to his apartment. We dumped him on his bed. The place was a wreck. The ashtrays were overflowing with cigarette butts. There were empty beer cans all over the rooms. A chunk of half-eaten pizza was the only thing in the refrigerator, and the door had been left open.

"We can't leave him or this place like it is," Carol said. She looked around, then sighed. "Let's get Coach cleaned up, then we can start on the apartment."

Digger cleared his throat.

"I think the guys should get Coach cleaned up and the girls should get the apartment cleaned up."

Terri folded her arms and glared at him.

"Do I look like a maid?" she snipped. "How come girls always have to do the sweeping and picking up?"

Digger shrugged. "Okay, you go get his clothes off and hold him in the shower. I'll sweep the floor."

Terri's arms dropped at her side. She kind of rocked back on her heels. "Oh, yeah." She spun and looked around at the rest of us. "Okay, here's the plan, you guys. The boys will get Coach cleaned up. The girls will get the apartment straightened." Then her eyes seemed to focus on me. "And Justine will call our folks and let them know where we are."

I jerked.

"Me?"

Suddenly, every eye was glaring at me.

"You," the whole team seemed to call out in unison.

"This was your idea," Buck said. "You call!"

*   *   *

I didn't want to. Trying to explain to Mama and Daddy why we'd slipped out of the house, trying to explain why I'd taken my little brother to almost every bar and beer joint in town, trying to explain why, instead of coming home, we were giving a drunk a cold shower and cleaning up his apartment—well . . . there was going to be more heat off this deal than anybody could stand.

Still, it *was* my idea.

While everybody else started on their various tasks, I found the phone under a pile of old newspapers and called home. Mama cried and told me how scared and worried she'd been. I had just gotten her calmed down enough so I could explain where we were and what had happened when the front door to the apartment burst open.

Daddy, Mr. Tate, and Oscar's dad flooded in. I could tell what a panic they were in—how worried they were about us—by the way they sort of tumbled over one another, all three trying to come through the door at the same time.

"Your dad and some of the other fathers are out trying to find you," Mama said.

I swallowed the lump in my throat. "I know. Daddy, Mr. Tate, and Mr. Dodd just came in."

Daddy raced to me. His rough calloused hands shook when he folded me in his arms, and he almost cried when he glared down at me. He stood, trembling, while I told Mama *everything!*

When I finished, she told me she'd call the other moms and tell them where we were and that we were safe. I hung up the phone and turned toward Daddy.

"I'm sorry," I whispered.

Daddy sighed. "I don't know whether to hug you or bend you over my knee and blister your seat." Then a gentle smile came to his lips. "I got enough of the conversation with your mother to know where you guys have been. I don't think you showed very good judgment, but . . . well . . . your intentions were good. What can we do to help?"

It must have been right about then that Buck, Brandon, Digger, and Randy turned the shower on Coach Reiner. There was sort of a scream, then a string of curse words. I'd never heard words like that before, except the time when Daddy accidentally broke a statue he was sculpturing and didn't know we could hear him through the air-conditioner duct that ran from his shop to the living room.

Daddy's eyebrows went up. He turned to the bedroom and motioned the other two men to follow. "We'll take care of Paul Reiner," he announced. "You kids wait outside."

"I don't know why we have to wait outside," Randy grumped, "we've all heard words like that."

"Yeah," Brandon agreed. "Dad messes up a flower arrangement sometimes. You ought to hear . . ."

Terri got to her feet and started up the stairs. "I think we ought to go finish cleaning. They're so busy with him they won't even know . . ."

A set of headlights rounded the corner at the end of the block. Then another and another and . . . It looked like a caravan. The cars stopped in the driveway and at the curb across the street. The rest of our parents turned off the engines and the lights and streamed toward us. They checked their kids to make sure they were okay, then went up the steps to help.

"Ain't it something?" Randy sighed, looking over his shoulder at the garage apartment. "Two years ago, none of us hardly knew each other. Our folks didn't hang out together. Nothin'. Now look."

Terri sniffed and wiped her nose with the back of her arm. "Mama kinda gave up when my oldest brother got sent to jail. All she did was sit around

and watch TV. Now . . ." She sniffed and wiped
her nose again. ". . . even she's up there and . . .
and . . . and. . . ."

Kathy patted her on the shoulder. "We know,
Terri. We know." She hugged her. So did Melody.

After a while, we got tired of sitting around waiting. We decided to go to the convenience store,
three blocks over, and get stuff to stock Coach's
refrigerator.

"Maybe my dad will loan me the keys and we can
drive," Oscar suggested.

"I could steer," Buck said.

Both of them shot a sly smile at Brandon. He
didn't say anything. He just closed his eyes and fell
back against the step like he'd fainted. We laughed,
then went to get some money from our folks.

It was two in the morning when they let us come
back into the apartment. The place was spotless.
There wasn't a speck of dust and all the furniture
was straight. Clean clothes hung in the closet and
the refrigerator was full of food and Diet Dr Pepper. Our team and our parents crowded into Coach
Reiner's bedroom. It was a small room and we
stood packed together like cattle shoved into a
boxcar.

Coach lay on his back under the covers. His lips were a little purple from the cold shower. He lay motionless, staring at the ceiling.

We all took turns, telling him that we cared about him. Even our parents took turns, reminding him how much he'd done for their kids and how they cared about him, too. Mama told him about the school board meeting and how he still had a job.

Coach stared at the ceiling.

We talked to him some more.

Coach hardly even blinked. If it hadn't been for his chest moving up and down under the covers from breathing, he could have passed for a corpse. No matter what we said, no matter how long we talked about how much we cared for him and still needed him, all he did was stare at the ceiling.

Finally, Ruth got mad.

Ruth *never* got mad. She always had that sweet smile on her face. Even playing her heart out in the middle of a soccer game, she smiled and never lost her cool.

"Ruth think Coach Reiner be a ignot," she growled.

Everyone kind of frowned and looked at her. Nick was standing beside her at the foot of the bed.

"What's an ignot?"

Ruth's nostrils flared. "A ignot. A dumb-dumb."

Nick smiled. "I think you mean idiot, don't you, Ruth?"

"Ignot. Idiot. What difference? That Coach Reiner. Him forget where *me* is. Him look in Michigan, then look in bottom of beer can. Still not find. Him hunt all over place for his *me*."

Our parents looked a bit confused. We knew what Ruth meant. She shoved her way through the crowd and stood beside the head of the bed. Coach looked at the ceiling.

"Ruth not too good soccer player." She leaned down close to Coach Reiner's ear and spoke softly. "Afraid to play too hard or be strong until day Papa talk to Ruth about old-fashioned stuff like honor. Now, grandmother very sick. She probably die. Daddy fly to Japan to see her. Ruth want go, too. Respect for elders very honorable thing for Ruth. But if go, not be able to help team." She sniffed back a tear. "Ruth worry that she not play very good soccer if Papa not here to watch. But when I tell him this, he just laugh. He say he give Ruth honor. It present from loving father. Not take with him when he go away. It belong to Ruth, now, for always."

She wiped her eye with her thumb. No one in the room spoke. We didn't even breathe deep.

"Coach Reiner give Ruth rule number five. He show Ruth where *me* is. We need coach. We need good coach who not get drunk and who not smoke up our nose. But if Coach go away—if Coach not come back—Ruth still have rule five. Rule five right here." She jabbed her finger against her chest. "Rule five stay here and no one ever take away."

Crying, she spun and forced her way toward the door.

"Ruth want coach," we heard her cry. "Ruth want team. But not quit. Never say quit. If have to, me play other teams all by self!"

There was a second of silence, then Digger Zimmerman stepped beside Coach and pointed at himself.

"Me, too!" He followed Ruth to the door.

Each of us did the same, and left Coach Reiner staring at the ceiling.

It was three-thirty when we left for home. I had no idea how late it was until Daddy turned on the car lights and the clock flashed. We were about five blocks from our house when he leaned over.

"What's that rule-five stuff Ruth was talking about?" he asked.

"It's the rule about not quitting," Nick answered from the backseat.

"But what does it mean?"

I opened my mouth to answer, but nothing came out. There was no way I could explain rule five. There was too much to it even to start to explain. I couldn't find the words.

CHAPTER 24

Coach Reiner didn't show up for practice on Monday. We only drilled for about fifteen minutes. We were so tired and sleepy after staying up all night we figured it would be best to go home and get to bed. We did agree that the game Sunday after next was the most important of the whole season. To make the state finals, we had to win. Mostly, we all *wanted* to beat the Hot Shots. So we decided to practice every afternoon, instead of every other.

On Wednesday, Coach showed up. He didn't come to the bench. Paco spotted him hiding behind the bleachers on the far side of the field. He had walked to the field instead of driving. He had a Diet Dr Pepper can in his hand instead of a beer can, and he was chewing on a soda straw instead of a cigarette.

We wanted to go talk to him. Kathy talked us out

of it. She said coming back was something *he* had to do. We ignored him and kept practicing.

Every day, on the way home from school, Digger checked the trash cans behind Coach's apartment. Every day he reported that there were no beer cans to be found.

Every day, Coach hid behind the bleachers and watched us. Every day, he drank his Diet Dr Pepper and chewed soda straws.

Every day—for two weeks—it was the same.

We played Paula Liven's Hot Shots at two o'clock on Sunday.

They were the cream of the crop. As Coach had reminded us a long time ago, most of them had played together since kindergarten. Leslie had told me they had a professional trainer from Dallas. They had new, sparkling uniforms.

And we were a bunch of losers. We were the misfits nobody wanted.

When the whistle blew for the half, we were ahead two to one.

We collapsed in front of our bench. While the others ate oranges and drank water, I looked across the field.

Coach Reiner was hiding behind the Hot Shot team's bleachers. The game must have made him nervous, because instead of drinking his Diet Dr Pepper and chewing his soda straws, he was chewing on his pop can.

As I watched him, peeking around the corner of the bleachers, I didn't see a fat drunk who smoked too much. I didn't see my old principal that I had in elementary school. All I saw was a man. Just a plain ordinary man who made mistakes and who felt sorry for himself and who laughed and cried and who, sometimes, just didn't know what to do.

Slowly, I got to my feet and went to join my team.

"Thomas Sikes is a little slow when he cuts to the left," Buck explained. "If we run the give-and-go play, I think we can get it past him."

"I know how we can get Coach back," I said.

Nobody seemed to hear me.

"But Leslie always comes to back up Thomas," Melody said. "If we run the give-and-go on him and . . ."

"We do it quick enough," Buck interrupted, "I think we can get it between them and . . ."

"I know how we can get Coach back," I said, louder this time.

Everyone looked up at me.

"How?"

*   *   *

I'd just finished explaining my plan when the ref blew his whistle and motioned us onto the field. Terri held up a finger, asking him to wait just a little longer. He looked at his watch.

Nick scooted closer to me.

"You sure you want to do this? I mean, as long as I can remember you've hated Leslie Liven. We're ahead of the Hot Shots. We can beat these guys. But if we do what you're saying, we're gonna lose. Besides, it might not even work."

I looked at my grungy soccer shoes and nodded. "I know." With a jerk of my head, I motioned to where Coach Reiner was hiding. "In my whole life I've never wanted anything more than to beat the socks off Leslie. The only thing more important is . . . I mean . . . we just . . . ah . . ." I couldn't explain it. I couldn't find the words to tell them.

The ref blew his whistle again. Buck got to his feet. He reached out a hand to help me up.

"Chocolate chip cookies," he said. When he pulled me to my feet, I was only inches from his face. His eyes caught mine and held me.

"Chocolate chip cookies," I agreed.

Nick shook his head. "What's this stuff about chocolate chip cookies?"

Buck blinked and his eyes released their hold on me.

"My grandmother fixed chocolate chip cookies for after the game," he told Nick.

"So?"

"So, whether we win or not, it doesn't make any difference. We still get chocolate chip cookies. She makes real good chocolate chip cookies."

Shaking his head, Nick went to the field. We all followed.

For the first five minutes of the second half, we played tough and hard. Melody got a breakaway and almost scored on them. Their goalie got lucky and blocked the shot. When he punted the ball, Brandon intercepted it at midfield and passed it back to me.

I trapped the ball with my foot and at the top of my lungs, I screamed:

"DRILL!"

Then I passed the ball to Nick.

"Jerry's dog?" he yelled, and passed the ball to Jerry.

"Barkus!" the whole team answered.

"Randy's math grade?" Jerry called and passed the ball to him.

"A-plus!" we all shouted.

"Melody's mom?"

"Lisa!"

"Occupation?"

"Barmaid!" There was pride in Melody's voice when she answered with the group, then passed the ball to Digger.

"Digger's oldest brother?"

"Denny!"

"Occupation?"

"Doctor!"

Ruth trapped the ball when Digger chipped it to her.

"Where is rule five?"

The second she asked that, the whole team froze in their tracks. We didn't move a muscle. Our three subs on the side of the field jumped to their feet.

We all looked to where Coach Reiner was hiding behind the bleachers.

Leslie Liven kicked the ball from under Ruth's foot and raced down the field. No one went after her. No one moved. She shot.

Terri leaned against the goalpost and didn't even watch the ball as it slammed into the net.

The ref put the ball at center field. He blew the whistle for us to kick off.

"Buck's dad?"

"Jeb!" we all called back.

"Paco's citizenship?"

"Mexican!"

"But soon be real American," we heard Paco call from the sideline. "Papa go to night school. Study hard so he can past test. Then we be good citizens."

"Ruth's favorite food?"

"Spaghetti!"

Oscar Dodd passed the ball to the other team. "Where's rule five?"

We froze. The Hot Shots dribbled down the field. When no one tried to stop them, when no one tried to block them or intercept the ball, they sort of hesitated. Then they drove in and shot.

Now the score was 3–2.

Coach Reiner ducked farther into the shadows behind the bleachers.

We kicked off again. We ran and passed and called out our drill and when Nick shouted, "Where's rule five," we were behind 4–2.

When Terri, leaning against the goalpost, watched their fourth shot trickle over the goal line and into the net, my plan finally worked.

Coach Reiner appeared at the side of the bleachers and walked toward us. We ignored the ref's whistle and his demands that we kick off.

We marched to the sideline and waited for our Coach.

He pointed at himself—at his chest. "Rule five's right here," he said. "Now quit this stupid drill stuff and beat these guys."

"If we're gonna have a soccer team," Randy said, "we're gonna need a coach."

Coach nodded.

"All right."

"It's gonna cost you," Buck smiled. "You've taught us a lot. Now we need a coach who can *show* us stuff. That means you're gonna have to get in shape so you can get on the field with us."

"Yeah," Kathy agreed, "and we're gonna need a coach who doesn't drink."

Coach shook his head. "I wish I could promise you that. I can't. I'll probably fall off the wagon again and if that happens . . ."

"If that happen," Ruth smiled, "it be okay—so long as you try. So long as you not forget rule five."

Coach patted his chest. "I not forget. Now let's play soccer. Let's beat these guys!"

Buck made a chip shot from thirty feet out. It bounced in over the goalie's head. The score was 5–3.

Melody slipped past the Sikes kid on a give-and-go. The score was 5–4.

Terri made another diving save. It was still 5–4.

The scoreboard clock showed thirty seconds left when Brandon cleared the ball downfield. Buck got it and broke for the goal.

CHAPTER 25

"I'm sorry," Buck apologized to me for about the seventh time. "I saw the goalie moving to the left. I should have shot to the right side of the goal. If I'd just made that one shot, we could have tied the score at five all and gone into overtime. If I'd just made . . ."

"Oh, shut up." I smiled. "Here. Have another chocolate chip cookie."

I stuffed the cookie in his mouth and laughed.

We had been a little down when we came off the field. Coach Reiner was laughing and drinking his Diet Dr Pepper. He told us we'd played a great game. We almost beat them, and winning wasn't important. What was important is that we didn't quit.

While the Hot Shots patted each other on the back and congratulated themselves, we sat around by our bench and ate the chocolate chip cookies Buck's grandmother brought. Our parents joined us, and even though we lost the game 5–4, we felt *great.*

As we were finishing up the last few cookies, we heard car tires squealing on the road. Everyone looked up. Jerry's dad was speeding toward us. I hadn't even noticed that he'd left.

At the parking area, he slammed on the brakes. His car fishtailed and slid. The front tires bounced over the cement parking block. Mr. Tate leaped out, left the door open, and sprinted toward us.

"I just got off the phone with the soccer association," he panted. "Noble just beat Lawton."

Nobody moved. Mr. Tate started jumping up and down. "Didn't you hear me? Noble beat Lawton."

Jerry got up and grabbed hold of his father.

"Calm down, Daddy."

Coach got up and shook hands with him and everyone gathered around.

"What Mr. Tate is trying to tell you," Coach explained, "is that Lawton lost to Noble, the Hot

Shots, and to Norman. They've lost three games. We've lost three games. That means we're tied for third place. We're going to state."

Chocolate chip cookies flew in the air. Pop cans flew in the air. Even a jersey or two went airborne.

We were going to state. We had another crack at the Hot Shots.

For the next three weeks, we trained hard. Every day after school, drills, running, more drills, new plays.

Coach Reiner worked hard, too. He came out on the field with us instead of sitting on the bench yelling out things for us to do. He did the drills with us. He showed us a trap-spin-reverse. He taught us a fake, where you act like you're gonna kick the ball only you just barely miss it and pass it the other direction with your other foot. He even ran to Parsons' Corner and back with us.

Getting in shape was probably harder on him than not drinking. The first couple of times he tried to run with us, he had to stop. When we noticed he wasn't with us, we went back and found him on all fours, throwing up in the bar ditch. He didn't want us standing around. He told us to go on. We jogged, slowly, so he could catch up with us. The second week, he got sick again. But he didn't drink. He didn't smoke. He didn't quit.

The week after school was out, we went to the state play-offs in Oklahoma City.

Saturday morning, we beat Norman. Sunday afternoon we beat Lawton. Sunday night, on the big field under the lights, we played the Hot Shots.

Ruth was our Oklahoma twister. She played hard until the Sikes kid kicked her knee on a slide-tackle. It was intentional. The ref red-carded him and put him out of the game. Ruth's knee puffed up like a watermelon. Paco took her place.

Then, Brandon and the Hot Shots' Daniel Steele were both going for a high pass. At the exact same moment, they jumped and tried to head the ball. When their heads cracked together, it sounded like someone shot a gun. They had to be helped off the field. Carol Quinton took Brandon's place.

The Hot Shots had a full roster. They still had six subs. With two of our kids out, we had one. Coach Reiner ran us in and out the best he could. He tried to give us a chance to catch our breath.

There was ten minutes left in the first half. The score was o–o when Leslie broke for the goal. Somehow she got around Nick. I dropped back from my position and got between her and the goal. She flipped the ball high with her toe and dodged behind me. Without even thinking, I reached up and swatted it down with my hand.

The whistle blew. I dropped to my knees and buried my head in my hands.

"Handball inside the box," the ref announced. "Penalty kick."

There was nothing Terri could do.

The score was 1–0. I felt rotten. Terri told me to blow it off and get back in the game.

Then, with thirty seconds left on the clock, Leslie got another breakaway. Nick got the ball, but Pete Leichter was following Leslie and got it back from Nick. He passed to Leslie and she shot.

Terri made the most fantastic save I ever saw in my life. She jumped from the right goalpost clear across the goal to block the shot at the left side. Only, she hit the goalpost when she slid. There was a loud cracking sound. The ball rolled back on the field. Instead of leaping up to cover it, like she always did, Terri just lay there. Pete Leichter shot it in.

We all ran for Terri. The scoreboard buzzer hummed, signaling the half. We huddled around

Terri. Coach shoved us out of the way and carefully helped her up.

Terri's arm bent at the wrist—so did mine. Terri's arm bent at the elbow—so did mine. Halfway between the wrist and elbow, Terri Jarman's arm bent again.

"It's broken," Coach told Mrs. Jarman when we brought her to the sideline.

Daddy jumped up from his lawn chair.

"I'll get my car, Judy. Baptist Hospital is only about three miles from here."

Judy Jarman helped her daughter toward the car. We watched for a moment, then one by one, we collapsed in front of the bench. We were beat. We were exhausted. We were dead.

We lay there, gasping for air. We were too exhausted to even think about eating an orange or drinking water. After a while, we got up and moved toward the water jug.

We fell into our circle around Coach Reiner. I guess we were expecting him to give us a big pep talk. We waited for him to get us all fired up for the second half. He just sat there, chewing on his straw.

Suddenly there was a commotion behind us. Terri came storming back toward the bench. Her arm dangled limply at her side. I could tell by the little puddles of water at the bottom of her eyes that the pain was killing her.

She stopped at the ice chest and opened the lid with her left hand. Then she sat down beside it and put her broken arm on top of the ice.

"Terri," Coach called, "you go get that arm taken care of."

Terri didn't answer. She just sat there with her arm in the ice chest. I could see that defiant, determined look in her eye.

Coach started to get up and go to her when Judy Jarman intercepted him. "We had a long talk at Mr. Smith's car," she explained. "Terri wants to stay for the end of the game. She'll go to the doctor as soon as it's over."

"But she's got a broken arm," Coach pleaded.

Mrs. Jarman smiled. "I know." Then with a jerk of her head, she motioned to her daughter. "But I ain't about to move her out of that ice chest. I've seen that look in her eye before."

Coach studied her for a moment. We'd all seen that look. At last he smiled and gave a nod. "Soon as the game's over, we're going."

He came back and sat down with us again. Ruth Osako limped over. "I ready to play again, Coach. Leg all better."

Her knee was still puffed up and she could barely walk.

"Go sit down, Ruth," Coach said.

"I'm ready to go back in," Brandon called from

the bench. Only, when he tried to get up, he sort of wobbled back and forth and had to sit down.

We waited. Coach didn't say anything. There were no words of wisdom, no sneaky, fantastic plays for us to try. Just quiet. The ref blew his whistle and motioned both teams back to the field. Coach still didn't say anything.

Finally, he made a grunting sound and got to his feet. "Justine, you take Terri's place as goalie. Kathy, you're at Justine's right halfback spot."

I fell back on the ground and covered my eyes with my hands. "Don't put me in the goal," I whined. "I can't do it. I'm not any good."

"You got quick hands," Coach smiled. "Now, let's go."

"What do we do, Coach?" Buck pleaded. "We're behind. We need some kind of sneaky play or something. We need . . ."

"You need something I don't have," Coach Reiner said softly. "I've had you run every play I know. We've got eleven players left—no subs. You're hot, you're hurt, and you're tired."

We all nodded our agreement, then stood— watching him.

"I wish I could give you what it takes to keep playing," he sighed, "but I already gave it away. Don't know where it is—not for sure. I do know that when you're tired and hurt, it's real easy to mis-place."

He folded his arms and rocked back on his heels. "I lost it myself one time. Thought my wife took it when she ran off with another man. Thought my old soccer coach had it in Michigan, only it wasn't there and neither was he. Thought that I could find it at the bottom of a beer can, but all I found there was empty. I do know that I couldn't find it out there." He spread his arms apart as if to encompass the whole world. "I couldn't find it—out there—no mat-ter how hard I looked. So, maybe it's not 'out there.' Maybe it's . . ."

The ref blew his whistle again. The Hot Shots stood in their circle and screamed and yelled. They patted each other on the back and jumped up and down. They were fired up and ready when they broke and raced to the field.

The Misfits didn't give a cheer. We didn't shout or yell. We were tired and hurt and hot and sweaty. Instead of bounding onto the field, like the other team, we walked. But we walked with our heads high and a soft smile on our lips. The people in the stands and the other team probably thought we were a bunch of idiots because . . .

As we walked, each of us pointed at *me*.

Because, *me* was all we had left.

CHAPTER 26

I guess the Hot Shots figured we were beaten. I guess for someone who didn't know what was going on, that's the way we looked. We were quiet. We moved onto the field slowly.

When the ref blew his whistle for the kickoff, the Hot Shots were secretly laughing inside and probably already congratulating themselves on the win. They seemed practically asleep when Buck, Melody, and Carol exploded down the field.

Randy chipped the ball over their forwards and halfbacks. Buck controlled the chip and passed it to Melody. Then the three of them did a three-man-wave through the Hot Shot fullbacks and Buck shot.

The score was 2–1.

The trainer from Dallas was yelling at his team. His team was yelling at each other.

Usually we cheered, high-fived, and patted all our teammates on the back when we scored a goal. This time, there was none of that. Our players walked quietly back to their positions on our side of the field. Buck came almost back to the goal to whisper something to Nick. I couldn't hear it, though.

The second the whistle blew, Nick and Jerry sprinted toward each other. They crossed right in front of me, then raced up the sidelines. For an instant, it scared me. Nick and Jerry were our full-backs. They were supposed to stay back and help me protect the goal. Without their help . . .

Somehow, Melody and Buck got the ball away from Leslie. Instead of dropping it back and orga-nizing a play, Buck kicked it downfield as hard as he could.

No one on the Hot Shots' team had noticed Jerry and Nick. When they did notice them it was too late. They broke past the Hot Shot fullbacks just as the ball landed at the top of the goal box. Their goalie hesitated for an instant, then charged for it. That second was all we needed.

I'd never seen Nick run so fast. It was like he wasn't tired at all. He reached the ball just as the Hot Shot goalie leaped for it. A split second before his hands scooped it up, Nick flicked the ball to the side with his foot. Jerry got it. He didn't even shoot.

He just dribbled it into the goal and stood there panting and holding onto the net.

It was only seven minutes into the second half and we were tied with the Hot Shots, 2–2.

Then—for the next thirty minutes—it was a battle. The Dallas trainer moved the Hot Shots into a man-to-man defense instead of the usual zone. Each of our players was covered. They shoved. They pushed. They stood so close to our guys that it looked like they were in the same shorts. When one of the Hot Shot players began to slow down or tire, the trainer ran in a fresh player.

Thirty minutes, the ball went back and forth and back and forth. Neither team could get a clear shot. Neither team could break the tie.

There was one minute left on the scoreboard clock. Kathy broke free and Melody chipped the ball to her. The goalie made a fantastic save, knocking the ball over the goalpost.

Quickly, Buck chased after the ball.

I was the goalie. I had one of the most important jobs on the team—protect the goal. It was my responsibility—stay in the goal.

Buck placed the ball at the corner flag.

I was exhausted. My legs were sore and weak. I wasn't sure I could stand, much less run.

Buck backed up to take the kick.

I broke from the goal box and raced down the field. Where the strength came from, I don't know. I just ran. I sprinted as hard and fast as I could.

There were forty-four seconds on the clock. I crossed midfield.

Buck raised his hand. Our team scattered, charging for the nearside and trying to get open.

The scoreboard clock flashed:

35. 34. 33.

I ran harder.

Buck glanced up one last time before he drove his foot into the ball. I didn't even know if he saw me.

The ball sailed over our team. It sailed over the Hot Shots. It sailed right to me. I caught it against my stomach. The ball dropped to the ground—right at my feet.

Their goalie's eyes popped as big around as two hot-air balloons when he saw me there, alone. He leaped. Came flying through the air toward me and the ball.

I kicked.

A little squeak came from my throat when I put every ounce of strength I had left into my right leg. The POP that echoed across the field was as deafening as a clap of thunder.

CHAPTER 27

The Junior Soccer Association had had nineteen first-place medals made up before the competition. They lay in a nice straight line on top of a table at midfield in the big stadium where the state finals were played.

I glanced at them and sighed.

Ignot, I thought. That was what Ruth called Coach the night we all crowded into his apartment. Ignots, idiots—what's the difference? That's what we were.

We had to be a bunch of idiots to ever hope to make the state finals, much less win. Fact is, we were probably a bunch of idiots even to try to make a team in the first place. And the second half, when we were already exhausted and didn't have one single person left to sub—shoot, the odds had been impossible. If we had any sense at all, we would have quit.

A little smile tugged at the corners of my mouth. Then again . . .

A man in a gray pin-striped suit stood behind the table. He picked up a ribbon with a gold medal on the end.

"Now for the first-place awards."

The people in the stands were on their feet. They started clapping and cheering even before he began to read:

"Paul Zimmerman."

"Jerry Tate."

"Justine Smith."

"Nick Smith."

"Randy Black."

"Melody Bolton."

"Kathy Fields."

"Brandon Foreman."

"Carol Quinton."

"Ruth Osako."

"Paco Santos."

"Oscar Dodd."

"Terri Jarman."

"Dennis Rogers."

"And the first-place trophy for the Junior Soccer Association Under–14 State Champions goes to the coach of The Misfits—Paul Reiner."

The cheer from the crowd was deafening. But it sure felt good when that guy put the ribbon with the little gold medal around my neck. I forgot about how sore I was. I forgot how much I hurt all over. I forgot how grungy I looked and how bad I smelled.

I just felt good. Real good.